D0123749

THE BEGINNING

Ana's Odyssey

Mariana Gumm

Copyright © 2016 Mariana Gumm
All rights reserved
First Edition

PAGE PUBLISHING, INC.
New York, NY

First originally published by Page Publishing, Inc. 2016

ISBN 978-1-68409-356-4 (Paperback)
ISBN 978-1-68409-357-1 (Digital)

Printed in the United States of America

THE BEGINNING

*I don't live in the past. I use it to push me forward
to the future.*

Ana

We come into the world when we, either by a twist of fate or simply by accident, are born as a small, innocent human being. The new person is totally vulnerable and helpless, stretching her arms as if to hold on to something or someone to provide for her survival. Her small brain is like a blank notebook, constantly assimilating knowledge and building memories moment by moment from everything occurring in her environment.

The circumstances of the infant's origin will mark her beginning on the road of life. The feelings of the parents at the precise moment of the infant's conception, though the parents do not imagine something like that happening, may very well determine the infants' perception of life. Completely dependent on her mother on instinct and her father out of necessity, the newborn begins to look over her world and internalize the care that is given to her and quickly learns on a very basic level what feels good and what is needed to survive. One of these necessary elements is love or affection gleaned from the way in which her needs are met. Consequently, her emotional development starts from the first moment of her creation.

Currently, there are few statistics on the topic of conception; few speak of the purpose of human life or of the role of a new being in this world. There are many parents who think that childbearing is the solution to their own needs for affection, acceptance, or as a substitute for affection they did not receive from their parents. With this mindset, the new parents focus on thoughts of the new being, which they have conceived will be a compensation for what has been missing from their lives. These parents are hoping the newborn will become an investment that fulfills their needs both present and future. Such parental hopes of compensation by the newly born will, for better or for worse, mark her future.

Every human being is born with the instinct for survival as is every other living being. The genetic heritage of her parents and her intelligence determine much of her character. Her life strategy is based on her satisfying her primary needs. It is here that the struggle between the ego and the superego, the struggle to be one's self or to please and be accepted takes place; life becomes a survival of the fittest. The baby begins her life's education by watching what others like and dislike. As she matures, she reviews her experiences and chooses what benefits her, what will make her either complacent and obedient or accepting of the consequences of being her authentic self.

Claiming her uniqueness or pretending to escape the reality she has chosen leads her to many uncertainties. Here the making of choices begins the life game of trial and error. Her reality begins to be dictated or shaped by everything that surrounds her as she moves through the years to come. The little one develops her fantasy of what she would like to be, but brothers, fellow playmates, school classmates, teachers, family, and religion will really shape her new image. If the new image is acceptable, positive, strong, and safe, the child will have a brilliant future. However, in many of the cases, the result is weakness, negativity, insecurity, and rejection. These negatively affect self-esteem and change personal values to unacceptable, negative, and unsafe. As a result, the unique, original, and authentic being has been consumed by forces of others. As life choices are made, the conflict between positive and negative begins, and the outcome determines the success or failure of the aspirations of that new life.

Inhibition and Doubt

During the second year of life, an infant begins to discover that there is more to her world than her crib and her mother with whom she has remained all this time. The infant discovers that there are other people trying to communicate with her. During this time in her life, she begins to carefully watch people's facial expressions, to hear the tone of their voices, and to judge others reactions to these actions. Through these observations of others, she discovers that she is related to the environment that surrounds her. In addition, at that moment, she realizes that she is not just a member of a family; she begins to see that there are people in her world besides her mother and her father. By adding facial expressions to both voices and tone, she begins to expand her mind with experiences. Based on what information comes to her world, she begins to imitate what brings positive responses and delete what is counterproductive. She looks for the acceptance of others by choosing what is more functional and by blending those new behaviors with her own currently held behaviors. The child, at this age, begins the exploration of what thoughts, words, and actions will be accepted or rejected. As her experience grows and her world widens, her brain registers those actions that will give her a reward and those that may cause her problems. With the growth in these areas eventually comes success and happiness as well as shame and doubt that sets the foundation of her self-esteem.

When the baby begins to take her first steps, her brain also changes. This stage of life begins the age of exploration of the outside world. So it was for little Ana who is trying to explore her environment. She tries to climb out of the chair in which her mother keeps her tied up so she does not fall. Ana keeps struggling and finally manages to break her bonds and tries to get on another chair. Her frustrated mother cries out, "Ana, get off that chair!" The little one, not seeing her mother's words as a reprimand, then thinks that she has been issued a challenge and climbs again. Mother's reaction is "Ana! What's wrong with you? Get in your chair." Her mother's tone of voice increases. Her mother's face turns red, and her lips tighten. Her mother's neck grows taut, and her mother grabs Ana by the arm as if she were a rag doll. "If you do it again, you will be sorry!" The toddler, at that moment, does not understand why her mother is so angry and threatening. The infant does not associate the words and the visual clues of her mother with the reprimand her mother intends. For Ana getting down from her chair and climbing into another is just a game, but she begins to realize that the game seems to be a big mistake. However, for Ana, it remains a challenge, something to test her own persistence.

Ana did not know, did not understand, that she could fall and hurt herself. Ana hears her mother's anger but does not register the anger just the message: "My mom does not like me." This notion causes her world to fall apart; she feels worthless and broken. All little Ana wants from life at this stage of life is to be loved, to be safe and to be accepted as she is. It is beyond the scope of her understanding that her mother wants her to be safe, that her mother may be tired or frustrated while dealing with other aspects of daily living. Ana wonders what she might have done to make her mother push her away. Each moment raises more doubts and brings on more uncertainty, more confusion as to what is not right? Since Ana cannot form meaningful insights because her thinking processes have not developed to that level, Ana only sees rejection and a lack of love. Ana hears the scolding words when she expects words of endearment. She expected affection and patience, to be lovingly taught what it is right or wrong, not to endure violent outbursts. With enough scolding, with enough anger, with enough doubt, her worth diminishes while her shame and guilt (though she does not know the words for the feelings she has) slowly increase until finally Ana believes that she is no longer a good person.

Ana has begun walking the path of low self-esteem. Her view of life is reflected by a clouded mirror that is no longer sparkling clean when once it reflected a clear image. Now the mirror only reveals hazy, distorted image. In the overall scheme of things, this little negative incident that for others may be insignificant, figures prominently for little Ana into the acceptance or rejection of herself by herself. The seeds of self-doubt have taken root and have begun to germinate in the fertile soil of her mind. If left to grow, these plants will affect her future decisions and, tangentially, her intelligence. Whether her garden produces the weeds of self-doubt or the flowers of self-esteem whether her future will be marked by the dried twigs and leaves of failure or the sunny landscape of triumphs is now being determined.

Ignorance and Poverty

Ignorance and poverty are often the seeds of misery and calamity. They can create chaos and instability. They can be the root of many diseases, both physical and mental, and consequently can erupt into social problems.

In many countries like Mexico, being born female would predispose the baby to less opportunities in society. One of the earliest signs of such a lower social status is the belief that a surname can only continue through sons. A prime example occurs when women, upon marrying, lose their surname and take the surname of their husband. In most cultures, for a couple to take a woman's surname rather than for the couple to take the husband's surname is viewed as breaking the continuity of the dynasty of the man of the house. Many people who strongly advocate the taking of the husband's surname in marriage hold fast to the idea that the surname makes the person. It would be very interesting to hear the response of such people when asked to give the last name of God or the last name of Jesus. Actually, what makes such a question irrelevant is that the answer is never mentioned in any book of the Holy Scripture.

A further idea of a naïve man is that he wants the male child to resemble him. Without even suspecting or perhaps even knowing that, according to the theory of genetics, there is a 75 percent chance that the male child will look more like the mother while the female child might look like her father. Regardless of an individual's origin or social class, the surname is really just a name. However, when the man tries to find himself in the features of the male child, what he really seeing is the image of his wife reflected in their beloved male children. While a recipient of his love and acceptance, the daughter is really the child who usually inherits a father's character and, in many cases, his physical features.

Another reason and another big myth about women is that they generate more expenses than revenues. The macho or patriarchal man always hopes to have his image reborn through his a male heir. These are consequences of some men's ideas that only men produce profits while women only produce debts. When a wife gives birth, her husband's first concern is whether the child is a girl or a boy. The new father is more concerned about learning of his child's gender instead of asking if the mother and infant are okay. If the newborn is a girl, his first thought is to ask one of two questions, Is this another expense that I need to endure or Is this more money just thrown in the trash? This line of questioning is foolish because the newborn has no opinions on the matter or no choice in being begotten. A parent, when assessing the financial future of the family, must figure in the cost of the new life, and that it will be much higher if the daughter is born sickly. The parents who assess the value of a child in terms of dollars and cents shuffle the coins in their accounts, wondering how much money must be spent until the infant is capable of producing any profit! "Sacrifice" is the word and is tied to the question, "Is raising the child worth the effort?? Adults just do not think of a third consequence of caring for the infant, which is joining their poor needs with the needs of their child for the self-preservation of the clan. Some parents fail to consider there are persons who fail to consider the need to preserve the human species, provide unconditional affection or respect for the new life that they do not even dream about the idea that children are a product of love. If a person with good judgment and with awareness of life's complexities mentions these ideas, selfish people or egoists deem her/him crazy or an alien from another planet. They may even ask if such a person ate something that made her/him lose his/her mind.

The Prophecy Has Come True

In Ana's life, the problems previously described became more evident when little Ana was sick for the first time. Her father's comments about treatment came out as follows, "I said treatment by a doctor is a pure waste of time and money." Ana's father ignored the reality that a baby would became ill as part of her normal development. With little Ana's having fallen ill, the fear of spending time or money was stronger than the fear of knowing that the illness might worsen and become fatal. However, thanks to home remedies for stomach pain, the crisis soon passed. The illness was only diarrhea, and the baby's will to live aided her quick recovery. The parents discovered afterward that the cause of the illness was the baby's having drunk spoiled milk. Giving the daughter spoiled milk since there was no fresh milk for her was a matter of pride. The parents asking for fresh milk from neighbors or borrowing from compadres was considered embarrassing. To offset future embarrassment, the parents, instead of seeking help from neighbors and friends, would give Ana rice milk to drink. Carbohydrates from rice would keep her alive and help her grow. With that milestone passed, life continued as if nothing important had happened.

Shortly after this incident, the lady of the house had good news for her loving husband. She was pregnant once again! The joyful news gave the family a chance to recover from the error of having delivered a baby girl on the first try. They were careful as the process of the gestation continued so God would give them a *machito*, a boy. No one at that time and place thought that babies would need food, clothes, attention, and time as borne out by family and friends gathering and repeating the age old mantra, saying, "Where eats one, two can eat!" The saying was definitely true during pregnancy. After the birth, the mantra becomes a myth for a memory because the parents must then provide the child and themselves with a healthy and nutritious diet. The question of food and basic supplies in Ana's village was often, "Would there be enough?" If the family did not have enough or barely enough for the first child, how would they have enough to provide for the second? In these discussions, there was no complaint, only the simple answer found in two beliefs in simple religious faith—God will provide and God will punish us if we complain about our state of affairs! Looking back to the days and the people of her youth, it almost seemed to an adult Ana that the act of giving birth to children for succession was an act commanded by God. This idea resulted in the unspoken belief that instead of complaining about their lot and working to improve their lot, the people had to multiply, hoping that a family of greater numbers would improve their lot.

As the time of the birth drew near, Ana's parents believed that life has given them a new opportunity. The parents believed and told their friends that this time they will have a smart, strong healthy boy; at least, those were their wishes. The months went by, and the blissful day arrived. The child was born and two parental dreams came true, the baby was blond and male! Great joy infected the family. A dream had come true! The best news for the parents was that he was apparently well and strong. All the attention shifted from Ana to the newborn. Nevertheless, as with many babies, a few days after his birth, he became ill and his mother tried to cure him by using home remedies the same way that she had cured Ana. Unfortunately, the bottles of chamomile tea and other home remedies were ineffective. Helpful neighbors started offering comments like, "He must need some sun tan" and "Poor *guero.*" The infant quickly grew so weak that he looked like gelatin with skin as white as snow. After trying all the usual home remedies, the parents looked for other alternatives. That time, they would see the doctor.

Ana's parents gathered some money and visited the doctor. Following the visit at which the doctor prescribed some medicine and giving the parents the admonition to return in a few days, the beleaguered family returned home. However, after returning home, the guero's situation worsened. His worried parents decided to seek a second opinion, only to find out, after the second opinion, that the problem appeared fairly advanced, and the second doctor told them there was little hope for a cure. There was little else to do to save the guero.

Returning to the ranch, the family carried disappointment and sadness in their hearts and minds thinking their *guerito* would not survive. The blond boy was so beautiful, which made it difficult to accept the loss of the child and the opinions of the doctors. In the depth of their fears, the parents grasped at any hope and decided to look for alternative medicine. The argument that the boy is the least expensive child and will bring in more money to the house than the girl was conversely settled there, the guero was more expensive to maintain than little Ana.

Some people told Ana's parents about a miracle healer who had saved others from death. That healer lived in the recesses of the Sierra Madre that divided the two states of Nuevo Leon and Tamaulipas,

Mexico. With renewed hope for guero, the parents saddled the mules and prepared some necessities for the trip. The parents stripped Ana of her blanket of beads and pink squares to cover the guero. According to her parents, Ana would not need such things as much as the sick one. Ana would stay with her grandma for a change.

Several days passed in the visit to the healer before the miracle worker gave hope for life for the guerito. To complete the healing process begun in the mountains, the parents must pay a visit to the Virgin of Trickle to thank her for the guero's salvation. After prayer and the services of the healer, the guero's parents were a little more relaxed and much more hopeful. As the family traveled to the ranch, the parents got the brilliant idea that if the guero died, they should have the replacement. They immediately took action. It did not matter that the mother was quite weak from the delivery and the long journey. It did not matter that she was anemic and exhausted, but nature did not notice her physical state and spawned the spare. Days later, they arrived home with the revived guero. All their bodies reflected the fatigue of the journey and the malnourished lady was more visibly exhausted and very pregnant. No one was thinking about any complications in the child's recovery process of the situation. No one gave much thought that the lady might lose the spare or that the pregnancy could endanger her life. As time passed, no one thought to follow the recommendation of the healer to take very good care of guero after rescuing him from the clutches of death.

THE FAMILY CONTINUES GROWING

A few months later, the replacement baby was born. Although the guero survived his illness, the poor baby boy was so *enclenque,* "frail," that he could not even walk when his brother was born. The replacement came out as a *morenito,* as brown as his father, but nobody said anything. At least the baby was a *machito,* as his father had hoped. Now with two babies in diapers and no money to hire help, the family had to use the help available, which meant Ana because she was there. Her independence and her youth meant that her parents had to train her to care for her brothers. At feeding time, the boys were tied together side by side into their respective seats. Their mother would give them their bottles, and then Ana took over their care. Ana was barely five years old when she became her brothers' nanny. For her, it was fun to see how the younger one would finish his bottle first and take the bottle from the guero to finish his bottle. It was at such times that her brothers became her entertainment, and she forgot that she should be playing with other children.

Life had become a routine for Ana's mother after the trials and troubles with her three children. She was left with the traditions followed by the other women at the ranch. There was no one who would think of another way of life. Since most families were poor and ignorant, they only knew the routine—planting and harvesting crops and, in between, having children. Nobody would attempt to change the lifestyle because it broke with the traditions of the people. So between the moans and complaints of poverty and desolation, life continued. Between discussions of crops, weather, and local news,

Ana's parents, like most other families in their rural region, continued their career of multiplying. It was always the same story. Mrs. Igna had already resigned herself to her destiny of being a woman, barefoot, pregnant, and poor while Don Ira saw his destiny as proving that he could be as macho as the rest of the ranchers, measured by the number of children he could sire. In his mind, he would be stronger and more important, particularly if his wife bore him many sons. It did not matter that his children were full of lice and other parasites as well as sickly and malnourished. All the kids from the ranch were like that, and eventually they got better.

Some months later, Igna was pregnant and waiting to deliver another machito. Although the Doña Igna said that she hoped, as with each pregnancy, that her dream of having a girl with curly blonde hair, green or blue eyes, and skin as white as snow would come true, the reality was that what she delivered were all boys. The next baby was a boy born blond and pale to the delight of Don Ira. When people came to visit the mother and baby, they did not stop saying, "How beautiful. He looks like a cherub." Visitors even doubted, under their breath of course, that the baby was the son of Don Ira since Don Ira was brown, *muy morenito*. No one knew or understood the concept that there most certainly were fair-skinned ancestors in both families, and certainly, in Don Ira's lineage because it was well known that Don Ira's deceased siblings as well as his living sisters were fair-skinned according to stories told by those who knew his family. It was a known fact that Mrs. Igna's father was a descendant of fair-skinned Spaniards.

With of the newest member of the family's arrival, the other children, who already did not fit in the bed of wires, joined Ana, sleeping on the cold dirt floor with rags of their parents' blankets for warmth. Their parents, of course, continued to sleep in a decent bed of thick mattresses. The cherub cried all night and bounced the crib against the wall completing the picture of the happy family. In the morning, the lady would be sleepy and tired like everyone else because the cherub was very restless. The lady had to light a fire to cook breakfast, which required great effort on her part. Mrs. Igna would first set the fire and then try to light it, a feat requiring oil.

When that would not work, she would use wood chips as kindling, but wood chips were scarce. Finally, she would add bits of paper to some of the cascaras, wood chips that Ana had collected the previous day. After a cloud of smoke and a few tears, the fire caught. Ana often wondered over the years if her mother's tears were caused by smoke or caused by the family's sad fate. After the fire was started, there was the question of there being enough sugar to sweeten the tea without even thinking about a glass of milk. Just asking for milk or sugar sounded like an insult to the man of the house, who had the right to drink some milk if there was some. The children would have to accept a *pintadita*, a few drops of milk in their tea. There was no need to mention milk for lunch and dinner.

In the winter, the situation at the ranch was even worse. The water froze and formed a layer of ice on the cooked corn, which Ana was responsible for washing to grind prior to preparing the dough for tortillas. Ana's small hands would bend and hurt as her fingers twisted with the cold ice, but she finished the task or would not be fed. She had to earn her breakfast. After mixing the corn, Ana had to help grind the corn as well to make the tortillas, which would feed the family for the rest of the day. The entire process would take the whole morning. When she finished with the tortillas, she helped care for the children. In the evening, she had to bring water from the well or the creek for cooking and any additional family needs. There was no indoor running water on the whole ranch. As a result of her duties, Ana's hands were a disaster. They were dry and cracked by the cold. The only thing that would cure them was lard, which reduced the dryness and prevented bleeding. She learned early that lotions or creams made for hands were not affordable, thus the lard!

Nature and Parenting

Some psychologists and experts who work in the science of human behavior claim that people relate to and identify with those individuals who have complimented their needs for affection, emotional support, love, and acceptance. In Ana's life, there were very few people with whom she could identify or who would serve as role models and those few could be counted on the fingers of one hand with some fingers left over. Those few were Ana's maternal grandfather, her aunt Lolita, Nana, and her first elementary school teacher. Others whom she encountered were strangers, entering her world for better or for worse to test Ana's reactions. Many of those strangers were itinerant peddlers who went through the town by selling trinkets or traveling photographers, who gave her a treat if she sang a song or danced for them. Occasionally, they took a photograph of her, which her mother, upon receiving the picture, confiscated because Ana was not among her mother's favorite.

Ana's maternal grandfather, one of her favorites on her list of role models, had awakened her imagination with anecdotes and stories and tales of treasures. Grandpa's favorite phrase was "The one who has it, has it because it has cost him dearly, and he deserves it." Grandfather used to say that people have money because they work hard and know how to use the resources properly. He usually got up at 4:00 a.m. if it was the sowing, growing, or harvesting season; ate some breakfast; packed a few supplies in his backpack; and started work in the *milpa*, his field. At other times of the year, he would go to his *huerta*, his orchard, to irrigate and fertilize the fruit trees. In addition to the cornfields and orchards, grandfather had cows, goats, and swarms of honey for each season of the year. Grandpa's vast orchards included a wide variety of apple trees, peaches, oranges, pomegranates, avocados, and prickly pears, and it was the most comprehensive of the ranch. At his home, no one could miss the wattles hanging from the trim work of his house with at least a dozen cheeses and barrel-shaped pots of honey on the porch classified by season and types of flower. There were jars of fruit preserves on the shelves and *gorditas* from the oven. It was a real delight for Ana to visit grandpa's home since it was like visiting another world, a world far different from her home.

Grandpa, though he never went to school, had a basketful of common sense; he knew that loving what someone does for a living enriches not only the spirit, but also the pockets. Her grandfather was respected for his reputation as a maker of fortune, thanks to his talents. His best investment was to buy gold and silver. He was also the banker or loan officer of the ranch. His lack of formal schooling did not keep him from calculating percentages in his head and knowing on the spot how much his debtors owed him. People whispered that grandfather buried jars and bags of gold and silver, but nobody knew where or how he did it.

Among the favorite tales that grandfather told was the story of the "Treasure of the Cave." Grandpa would begin the story by saying that in a place far away from the well-traveled path, there was a cave from which sounds of ropes and chains can be heard at midnight. At the same time, a voice was heard saying, "All or nothing." One night, a hiker heard the noise and the voice but was afraid of it. He decided to tell his best friend and compadre about his fears and suspicions that there might be gold in that place. That tale aroused the compadre's ambition, which convinced him at first, that both should explore the place together. The two men would visit the site on the darkest night at the darkest hour, the night of next new moon. However, knowing where the cave was, the compadre's temptation to seek the treasure for himself was stronger than his friendship. Falling victim to his greed and avarice, the compadre decided to seek the treasure on the night before the designated date selected by his friend and him. When he approached the cave, he paused some distance away until it was fully dark. At the stroke of midnight, he heard the sound of chains and the voice saying "All or nothing."

The compadre answered," I want *all.*"

After the compadre's reply, the voice guided him to the treasure he so ravenously wanted. Out of the mists, the pots magically appeared right before his eyes, but they were sealed and heavy. The treasure was hidden from him. Carrying the pots to a safe place some distance from the cave, he immediately began to open them one at a time. As he unsealed each pot, he became more and more enraged. Instead of gold and silver coins, the pots were full of mud and animal waste. He assured himself that someone had played a terrible joke on him. In anger, the compadre, thinking his friend to be the culprit, decided to go to his friend's house and dump the pots over. His friend's house had a trap door, like a skylight, on the roof. With great effort, the compadre climbed onto the roof, opened the trap door in the ceiling and dumped all the big pots onto the homeowner's' bed, saying, "There it is. Enjoy your treasure!" The following morning, the homeowner found the nice surprise delivered during the night. The compadre, meeting the homeowner in the morning, asked the homeowner with a mocking smile, "And how did you wake up this morning?" The homeowner said to his compadre, "A miracle has occurred. Someone has left me a gift at my feet. Many gold and silver coins. I think someone went ahead of us to our cave, found the treasure, but didn't like what he saw! Here is a proof to what I am telling you." With that, the homeowner gave his friend some coins for being the best friend in the whole world. The moral of the tale is twofold: Morbid ambition always ends badly, and the reason someone receives the treasures in this life is that he deserves it."

Grandpa always told many stories and fables apart from the story of the treasures. He would also say that the women were so good to give birth in homes instead of giving birth as the hens do, "laying little babies in corn cribs or nests." He would tell stories that almost nobody would remember by the time he returned to his house, but nobody could imagine that these same stories had been engraved in Ana's memory as messages for the future.

The next person on the list of people who left an imprint on Ana's life was her aunt Lolita, the widow of Ana's uncle. Lolita was the healer, the clerk, and the artisan, who made clay griddles to provide for her family. She had three children, Tota, Nana, and Mago. Whenever Ana suffered from any type of affliction, she visited Lolita's house and asked her to make her a remedy. Depending on the symptoms of the illness, whether for *mal de ojo*, ear or flu infection, and the bad vibes, Lolita would prepare a remedy for Ana. For the mal de ojo, she would use an egg, passing it over Ana's entire body and offering complex prayers to the spirits. After finishing the ritual, Lolita emptied the egg into a glass of water to make the bad sprit go away as the egg and spirit dissolved in the water. Whether or not it was an effective remedy, for what it was worth, the ritual made Ana feel relieved. For the *espanto* (frighten), Lolita rubbed Ana all over her body with a broom made of the ash bush and from wild lavender while simultaneously chanting prayers of recovery of the spirit: "Spirit of Ana don't delay or get lost." To these words, Ana had to answer: "Here I go." For some rare reason, Lolita rationalized the Ana's illnesses resulted from Ana's being very perceptive of her environment. This trait would make Ana sick since most of people who surrounded her had negative energy. Perhaps, there was some truth to Lolita's theory. When Ana grew up, she was able to perceive people's vibes and energy faster than the rest of people she knew.

For the bad vibes, Lolita used the stone of fire, which was a crystal-like stone that she believed had healing powers. After passing the stone over Ana's entire body and praying, she burned it in the fireplace before Ana's eyes. Lolita told Ana that the stone, whose shape was always changed by the fire, had the bad thing. The thing, as Ana later learned, was probably Ana's childish imagination. For future protection, Lolita would give Ana a necklace with a brown ball called tiger's eye or the *ojo de venado*. Lolita said that brown ball would absorb the bad vibes. Since Ana was very sensitive to all types of energy, she constantly attracted very strong vibes, which would break the amulet. When Ana realized that the necklace had fulfilled its task and broke in half, Ana would run to Lolita's home for another. In addition to caring for Ana's spiritual illnesses, Lolita also took care of Ana's long hair. Sometimes Ana would go for days with her dirty and unkempt hair. Ana's mother had no time to comb it. It seemed only Lolita had the patience to wash and brush Ana's hair that was very thick and very long, making care a real hassle for Ana's mother.

Nana was Lolita's eldest daughter. She had grown up, and like many others from the village, she was working as a maid in the city. Whenever she came back to the ranch, she brought gifts for her family and for Ana. Since nobody gave anything to Ana, Nana wanted to give Ana her first doll. Unfortunately, Ana did not enjoy the doll for long. Ana's mother had taken it from her, so "she would not destroy it." Ana could only look with curiosity at her blue-painted happy-faced doll with its hair in a bun and sitting inside the box, kept on the highest shelf.

Several months after Ana received the doll, Nana visited her niece. She asked Ana if she still had the doll. Ana had no idea that the box with the cute doll was for her. Nana said it belonged to Ana, and seeing the box on the shelf, gave the doll to Ana. Nana asked Doña Igna why she had not given Ana the doll, and Igna replied that she did not want Ana to destroy it. Following the interchange, Nana took down the doll and Ana, with her aunt, played with the doll for a long time. Having such a beautiful doll brought much joy to the young girl. Ana so happy to have such a doll slept with the doll, hugging the doll as if it were the most precious treasure, which, of course, to Ana it was. The next day, Ana's mother asked her for the doll, and Doña Igna returned it to the shelf in the blue box. Whenever Ana wanted to play with the doll, her mother would give it to her only if her mother had time to watch, so Ana would not break it.

After a while, Ana's mother invented excuses to keep the doll from her, and Ana gave up asking her for the doll. One day while cleaning her parents' room and looking for something that had fallen under her parents' bed, she discovered the doll's head! With her face full of surprise and sadness and being unable to recall the last time she played with the doll, Ana ran to show her mother the doll's head. Her mother, instead of sympathizing, chastised Ana. "What did I tell you? Everything you touch, you destroy! There was a reason that I didn't gave it to you before." Ana could not understand the reason behind her mother's comment and walked away, hurt and confused. How could her mother have forgotten how much she loved and cared for the doll? How could she have dismembered the doll she liked so much? How could she have even thought of doing such a thing? The most bizarre piece of that puzzle was that the doll's body was never found.

After that incident, Ana learned to make her own toys. From the stems of the pumpkin leaves, she made flutes; from slats of wood, *rumbadores*; and from bags of paper and plastic, Ana made balls. Though she made the toys, Ana had little time to play with them or with other children because she had to care of her siblings. They became the dolls she never had. Little five-year-old Ana became the nanny, the cook, the maid. She helped with the cleaning and the milling; she brought water from the stream or well. She washed both dishes and her brothers' diapers. If she had a complaint or offered resistance to the orders, Ana would face dire consequences.

The Resignation

Ana's mother, Doña Igna, had her own, very peculiar, way of thinking. Leaving a home and family in which nothing was missing to follow her dream, Mrs. Igna eyes were quickly opened to a reality that smashed her dreams. She found her only choice was to resign herself to her new life, to accept the destiny she chose, and to "endure the rod," as husband Don Ira told her. She traded a home in which she had a father whom she must obey for a husband whom she must obey. She left a home with few chores for a home with duties and responsibilities. Her premarriage world offered multiple choices; her post-marriage world changed dramatically so that, at just thirty years old with a bunch of kids, Igna had no option but to continue to live in Don Ira's home and follow her destiny.

As she reviewed her life when she chose to reminisce, she realized there were few choices open to her. No one at the ranch, after all, could or would offer her an alternative lifestyle. All, or most, of the people she knew thought as she did due to the lack of resources and education. Many of the ladies in the village had not completed third grade or, in some cases, could not even write their names. As a result, they were trapped in a tradition that forced them to bear children and do work that has been described as a few steps above slave labor. The women just did not know any other way to survive. Igna, when she reminisced, always came to the same conclusion: there was no escape from her commitment to Don Ira. Each day was the same. She accepted her fate. She followed the orders and met the demands of the law, Don Ira who was the law. He thought—no, he knew—that he was always right. His voice was the authority, and no one in his house could discuss or criticize any of his ideas, no matter how far from reality they might be. If someone in the family dared to challenge them, the situation for that individual became quite unpleasant.

Not wishing to complicate matters further and wishing to continue surviving safely, Igna took as her "daily bread," Don Ira's orders. The first of these orders described her main duty: to bear him as many sons as possible, no matter the living conditions in which they lived. However, in her world of misery, Igna kept only one dream alive, to bear a blonde, blue-eyed, white-skinned girl. Keeping her dream a closely held secret, she would say to those who asked that God had not yet granted her wish, but God, at least, had given her gueritos, sons who diminished her guilt feelings for not having her wish fulfilled. Igna, having no confidence in talking of her thoughts and feelings to others, would talk with Ana, who became her mother's handkerchief for her tears. Igna may have believed that being her little girl, her chiquita, Ana would not remember or understand what her mother was telling her. What Inga did not know was that Ana had a memory like an elephant. Ana remembered almost everything. Although some of Igna's confessions were mean-spirited and hurtful to Ana's dignity or feelings, the one that hurt most was Igna's wistful dream of having a blonde girl with blue eyes. For Ana, Igna's confessions meant that Ana was not worthy of her mother's affection and acceptance.

Ana's failure to earn some affection from her mother despite Ana's constant efforts represented a major challenge and a greater source of emotional pain. No matter how often Ana was rebuked, she continued daily to pursue her quest for just even an iota of maternal affection to feed Ana's soul and spirit. It needs to be noted here that due to poverty and deprivation. A bit of affection might be the only thing that did not cost money, or so Ana's thought. Much later in her life, Ana learned that poor Igna was unable to deliver that maternal love or affection for one simple reason. Igna had never learned the full meaning of maternal affection because Igna's mother had died when Igna was a toddler. With her mother's death, Igna's mind and heart had frozen, causing her to become disconnected from any maternal feelings. Adding to her life of abject poverty, her lack of experiencing maternal love herself, Igna found it very difficult for to turn on the fire of maternal love, particularly when Ana was far from being the girl of her dreams.

AN INCLINATION
TOWARD POLITICS

Politics came to the ranch in the beginning of the 1970s. It was the election season for the offices of both the governor of the state and the president of the republic. As in most elections everywhere, it was customary for the candidates to campaign to collect votes. Campaign by each opposition candidates was more for show than real for social convention because everyone knew that the party in power would win because, for generations, candidates of the party currently in power always won. The most important part of any campaign for the rural poor came when the crew of the candidate, who was soliciting their votes, gave away food. The election season began with the gubernatorial candidate who gave milk powder to all the malnourished children at the ranch. Such a gift was seen as a beacon of light and hope that things would improve in the near future. As was customary, the packages of powdered milk were distributed according to the size of the family. Ana's family had a good chance of collecting a large portion of milk powder, which only confirmed Don Ira's theory that there is no evil that good doesn't overcome.

During campaign season, there were always changes, people wearing their best outfits, bathing and combing their hair to look their best, gathered at the local school to prepare a feast to welcome the candidates. For the school children who were actively involved in the local campaign celebration, it was customary to select a student from the class to read the welcoming speech. The teacher would choose the student who was a good public speaker and who was neither shy nor timid when appearing before important people, such as the candidate for governor of the state. For Ana, speaking in public was never a big problem, but Ana was six years old and not registered her in school, so she was ineligible to be the speaker Not being registered forced Ana to be creative in making arrangements to go to school as a listener. She would hide at the back of the classroom, so no one would notice her presence though sometimes the teacher would wonder what that girl was doing back there.

Since Ana could neither read nor write well in addition to being an unregistered student, Ana knew she would have to rely on a tool she had used on many occasions. Ana pulled her very good memory and willingness to help off the shelf. When the time came for the gubernatorial candidate's visit, the teacher chose a student who could read better than the other students in the class to welcome the candidate. Ana resigned herself to not delivering the welcome speech, but nevertheless, Ana had memorized the speech given by the selected student. On a hope and a prayer, Ana asked her parents to buy her a decent dress, even second-hand, and shoes since she only wore sandals. The idea she held in anticipation was that if the chosen student were not performing as hoped, Ana would jump to the rescue.

When the much anticipated day arrived, the ranch was ready and adorned. The program was ready; people were gathered to welcome the candidate and excitedly awaited his arrival. The children who would present the speech lined up in a row behind the curtains. Ana, in her new dress and shoes, stood hidden within the group. Ana, with her memorized speech, was placed behind the bandstand to await her time. The candidate arrived. With great pride, the chosen student of the school stood and walked to the podium; however, overcome by emotion, the original speech was forgotten and the chosen student began to stutter. Ana, stepping out from behind the class, came to the rescue. Ana decided to improvise. "Welcome Mr. Candidate to this ranch, this poor *arrabalero*, unpaved and full of muleteers, donkeys, and with much pride." The embarrassed teacher stopped the speech and pulled Ana from the stage. The candidate, however, smiled and thought that Ana was very funny. To validate her courage and effort, he gave her several notebooks and pencils. To Ana, the candidate's gift was more than enough of a reward because she never had a decent notebook. For Ana, getting those notebooks and pencils was like winning the lottery's grand prize. There would then be no excuse for not going to school, but her parents had other plans for her.

ANA'S PREDESTINATION

You do not prepare the path for the children, just prepare them for the path.

Popular Saying

Ana's parents had thought that they would use her to assist Igna since Ana did not complain about the house chores. The idea was that Ana, being female, could only become a housewife (if she would ever marry), and for a housewife, school was as a waste of time. The common consensus was that Ana did not need to go to school because she had better things to do at home. Ana thought otherwise. Ana was not resigned to the fate that her parents had outlined for her: caring for her siblings, helping with cleaning and other household chores, becoming a housewife and mother. Acting against her parent's plans for her, Ana escaped when she could to the local school. She would take her notebook, pencil, and small chair or *banquito*, and sit in the back of the classroom so as not disrupt the class. At the end of class, she was the first to leave the schoolroom, running quickly to avoid being *regañada*, scolded. Later at home, she could not avoid the consequences of leaving the children without care, and they would always need her for something. The tales of Ana's absence from the brothers quickly reached the family patriarch, and according to the law, she deserved a punishment. When she returned home, Don Ira was waiting for her with his belt in hand to give her what she deserved. If she escaped the next day, the parents hoped the marks of the belt would cause her shame when the other children saw her legs marked by the *cintarazos* that sometimes would break her skin and stay for a long time. Don Ira thought that the shame of being whipped, in addition to the whippings themselves, would convince Ana of the folly of her attending school.

However, for Ana, no human force or punishment could stop her. One day, the teacher, feeling sorry for her and rather than punishing her for attending school without being registered, visited her parents to talk about formally enrolling her in the class. Ana was fearful that her parents would think that she was causing problems for them at the school. When the teacher arrived at her home, Ana hid behind the door to listen to the discussion. After a long conversation with much give and take between the parents and the teacher, the teacher was able to convince her parents that knowing how to read and write properly would serve her well, and that she had as much right to learn to read as the rest of the children already in the class. During the meeting that evening, Ana recalled what she had told her parents on other occasions. She really would like to learn something in life, since what she saw to her surroundings was not pleasant at all. In addition, education would keep her from being as rude and crude like others. Her comments came from the reality of her thought that teachers know how to change the thinking of others. She knew that they could also help to change her life. However, it was not until her parents met with the teacher that her parents finally accepted the idea that Ana really wanted to go to school. Simultaneously, her parents said that if she attended school, they would not help her to avoid doing her chores. Ana would have to manage her time and tasks both at school and at home since that was the way things would be at this time.

THE SEVENTIES AND ITS CHANGES

With all that was happening in Ana's life, the state and the country awaited the election of the president of the Mexican Republic. The custom was for presidential candidates, like the gubernatorial candidates who traveled throughout the state, to visit the most faraway points of the country. That part of the political process was not new or demanding. The leading candidates, who knew that the majority of the population was poor and ignorant, believed it would not be difficult to convince the rural population to vote in his favor. As with any candidate's visit, the ranch was partying again. The poor farmers, often called peasants had been influenced by the ruling party to paint propaganda with murals and signs containing the three official party colors, green, white, and red. For even more signage, the poor farmers painted large ads on the hills and on the walls of what was called a road in the evening,

The signs said "Above the peasants, down with the chiefs. Vote for the PRI." Ana was curious, watching the efforts of the people as they worked to make the giant signs, and finally, she asked, "What does vote mean? No one could give a logical explanation, only showing her ballots that had circles of different colors next to the pictures of all the candidates. People told her that just by making a cross in a circle next to a candidate, they would elect the president. Next, Ana asked how the people knew if the candidate they voted for was the best for the country? The responses were the same, "Because he is in the party for the poor." The adults, after answering, told Ana not to ask any more questions and to wait to grow up, so she could better understand things. What Ana did understand was that the signs that the peasants painted would not last through the night. The offended chiefs would destroy them before sunrise. The following week, farmers painted them again. Ana wondered whether it really mattered how old the people grow because people always seem to squabble as children do.

The political season passed slowly, and days after the visits, Ana saw a few trucks full of gifts—particularly cookies—coming up the road. The PRI party candidate had won the presidency as expected. The new president's first gift was his way of sending greetings to the poor, cookies. That gift reinforced the idea that better times will always come, as Don Ira said. Many children in the family benefited from the president's charity since the more children a family had, the more boxes of cookies the family could collect. With so many kids at home, Ana's family could eat cookies until they burst. In fact, the family did not eat anything else for several days until the cookies were gone, and some Ana's siblings ate so many cookies that they suffered from indigestion.

Everyone at the ranch had voted for the PRI. Among those who returned ballots were children too young to vote as well as a few dead people who rose from their eternal rest to make their mark. The cookies and the political promises of abundance and better times to come had stimulated the only thing the people at the ranch were used to doing, making more babies, but did nothing for the local economy. To remind the local peasantry who had given them gifts, the newly elected president sent a photograph of himself with his beautiful family of ten children with their respective offspring and wives to all families at the ranch. That picture left no doubt in the minds of the local populace that the president was setting an example of the large family with many children. His was a very good example to follow. Consequently, many people imitated the good example of their president and continued having very large families. The few saw that having large families was a foolish and unhealthy idea. However, for the many, the idea of constantly reproducing offspring had been reinforced and clearly repeated by many fathers that having children was the best way to leave a mark on this world and ensure the people's legacy. Unfortunately, the legacy was one of poverty and its consequences.

Logic or common sense did not seem to exist at that time on the ranch. The people did not see that the president came from a lineage of highly educated people, of an old political family, as well as a family entrenched among the wealthy elite. Such families could have all the children that Mother Nature granted them because they had sufficient resources to feed them, clothe them and educate them. On the contrary, that was not the case for the ignorant peasants who had little or nothing to offer their malnourished and sickly children or to their malnourished and tired wives. The president had a strong and diverse income while the peasants' lands were becoming sterile and less and less productive each season. The rains did not come as consistently as they once did, and the people did not understand the idea of a drought. Since reality was delivering one hard blow after another to the innocent people of that rural area, particularly to powerless children, politics were of little consequence to a people who were thirsty and starving!

OVERPOPULATION AND MULTIPLICATION

The era of the seventies promised hope and prosperity when the new president, with his beautiful family, continued to convince the population, mostly the poor, that they could be as successful as he is by following his example. As a result, nobody, looking at his family's portrait, could think of any other thing but reproducing and having large families. They could not see or understand that the president was telling them to get an education, to get twentieth-century vocational training, and to work smarter to improve their lot rather than to simply enlarge their families. As people talked, misinterpreting the message, it seemed that no one could be happier than the men. As the men told the story that if the president has set the examples, then those who did not have money, people like the men at the ranch with nothing to lose, had every reason to continue fathering children. Everyone was on task. If a family had a child at least every two years, then they would have one a year and, sometimes, twins. It was no different in Ana's home. There was no debate and definitely no arguments especially when a person has nothing to lose but to work until they drop. As Don Ira said, "Don't be a coward."

Ana's parents were not married in the church due to their rush because they thought that it was better to start their family immediately rather than save for a future wedding. Looking back, how much could a wedding have cost, how long should the couple wait or postpone the wedding if the couple's love was strong and worth binding forever? Again, looking back in the case of Ana's family, especially for Don Ira, there was more of a need to have a woman in the house and to see that their offspring multiply than to see if the union could give them happiness. To have the marriage blessed came when opportunity knocked on the door as part of the changes for better life the government had implemented. The current government created a campaign of evangelization by proposing that people had to multiply as God commanded with the blessing of the church.

To make the evangelization all the more formal, several couples would receive the blessing in a group. As most of these families already had a lot of children, the women were not allowed to wear white but only to wear a decent dress. Mrs. Igna designed a dress in gray-blue, which was her favorite color. To Ana, gray-blue was the saddest color her mother could have chosen since it reflected only sadness. Ana kept her opinion to herself, rationalizing her decision by thinking. "So what? Who would care about the opinion of a seven-year-old girl?" When the day of the weddings arrived, the couples to be married gathered in one of the houses that the priest had chosen. The priest or padre gave them his blessing and sent them forth. After the ceremony, everyone returned to his/her own home with the hope that if they were now blessed, everything would be easier, and they could overcome all adversity. With six kids and a life full of troubles and poverty, Mrs. Igna and Don Ira believed that being married in the church would improve their quality of life through the art of faith.

Reality always slapped them down just like the winter wind cruelly tortures a bare face. A bit of that reality came through the actions of the smallest child. The rebel was always an angry cat, used to slamming his wooden crib against the wall with such force that, sometimes, it would hook on the wall, and the boy would roll to the ground. After crying for some time, he would sit in the doorway, alternately yelling and crying while waiting to be rescued. When the child was angry, he would throw a big tantrum, and sometimes, he would crawl around a room and crash his head against the wall. If the wall were some distance from his chosen spot in the room for the tantrum, he would drop his head on the ground and cry like a kid slaughtered. Given all the commotion, the whole people in the vicinity would run to see what was going on. Some visitors and neighbors would even ask his parents why the little one was so angry. One of the common questions to Don Ira and Doña Igna was "What are you doing with that poor child?"

Throughout all the turmoil, Mrs. Igna continued her routine while Ana continued her chores. It took the two of them at least half a day now to make tortillas for the whole family. At the same time, Ana had to assume the responsibility of caring for the small, rebellious child. It was very difficult and very frustrating for a seven-year-old girl without knowledge and experience to control a child as unsettling as her brother. Igna, whether from a desire to pursue other ventures or from a failure to understand her youngest son, continued to give the child to Ana. Igna's justification for giving the child to Ana to manage was that such work would prepare her for her later role in life as a properly trained housewife. Igna thought the training necessary because being a housewife was the only proper destiny for a young woman. Doña Igna hoped someone would do Ana the favor since the *pobrecilla*, "poor thing," had nothing to offer. Igna would teach Ana as much as possible, so *poor Ana* could learn how to deserve a man. As part of her training, Ana had to check the child for soiled diaper. If she found one, she had to report the mess to Lady Igna who would change it because Ana's hands were too little. After the diaper had been changed, Ana would have to wash it because there was no money to buy disposable diapers.

The little Tuito continued his tantrums almost nightly and awakened everyone at 4:00 a.m. His crying was uncontrollable and caused by many things, both large and small—he might be hungry, he might be dirty, or he might have colic. To the residents of the ranch, it was not uncommon to hear him crying at the top of his lungs at all hours of the day or night. Finally, tiring of the situation and, above all, to avoid the shame from gossiping neighbors, his parents decided they had to seek a solution to the problem. Since they could find no reason for the child's rebelliousness, they concluded that the child was probably *maloreado*, meaning the child had lost his soul. With that illness decided, the parents sought a cure for the child from the local healers. However, the healers of the rancho could not fix the angry child. They told the parents that it was probably best to take him to the nearest holy saint. For the family, that was San Francisco de Assisi. They were to promise him an offering. They made plans for the trip, including setting aside the finances necessary for the journey and for the offering. That time, nobody in the family or in the village thought the trip was a big sacrifice because the angry child was a valuable asset, being a machito and guerito, a blond boy. To make the journey, the parents sold the pigs and the chickens to raise enough money for the trip. Only the parents and the rebel would make the trip; the rest of the family was left at home to survive on whatever they could find, usually just beans and tortillas.

The couple gathered up their money and provisions and made ready to travel with their offspring with the faith that the saint could cure him or at least calm him down. They also hoped that, after the pilgrimage, the child would speak clearly since nobody understood him now when he tried to speak. After a few days at the saint's shrine, the happy family returned with the child partially cured. Since then, at least, he was speaking a few understandable words. That alone was a relief since he could tell everyone what he needed or why he was so annoyed when he threw tantrums. Looking back, it never occurred to the parents that the child had inherited the character and genes of his father since Don Ira's only solution to anything was some type of physical violence. He only used violence with his children because Don Ira would never challenge someone his size, a very perceptive insight from Tuito when he was able to give a voice to the idea.

THE OVERPOPULATION
AND SHORTAGES

The government, in the wake of severe food shortages and, in some parts of the country, water shortage, had finally realized that they had misled the people, or perhaps the people had misunderstood their message, by allowing the population to reproduce like a fashion sport which had contributed to the shortages. The demographic explosion had accelerated like a rocket that was launched. At the same time, the drought sharpened and significantly reduced food production. More people, less food and less water meant that hunger expanded throughout most of the nation. The government, in reply to the crisis, implemented different programs of social awareness. The first strategy was to increase the self-esteem of women, so they could start to focus on using their brain in a more efficient manner. The International Year of the Woman was born as their answer to the nationwide problems. The right of voice was now given to the woman, but men still thought that women would only waste their time by following the new proclamations. When the first part of the program was implemented, that liberation movement did not sit well with the men. The government planned that if awakening the submissive and obedient woman worked, the second part of the plan would be implemented, to awaken the husbands to the new reality. The first step meant that the government had to wake up the woman from they called her "state of being an automaton." The women had to abandon their old role of being blindly obedient, tragically resigned to doing everything that the man demanded. The message being stated somewhat indirectly, almost subliminally, told the women that they had to say no to the male-dominated need to multiply. The media, through radio programs and songs that described the new roles of men and women, worked to remove the women from the dark night of her submissive world and blind devotion to tradition. At the same time, the program promoted the husband's awareness of his primary role as a provider and protector of the family in a conscientious and efficient manner.

Social workers spread out to the far-flung villages and ranches to teach classes on the proper use of contraceptives and distribute brochures on the care necessary for having healthier children. They also taught the poor that a small family lives better. To complete the picture, an agricultural worker taught classes on modern gardening methods, modern farming methods, and the proper planting of some healthy and vitamin-rich vegetables for a basic food basket. The idea behind the push for teaching better gardening techniques was to ensure that the family, as the basic unit of a good community, should be well fed. Everything sounded quite good, the only problem that would slow down the changes or keep them from happening at all would be the resistance of the uneducated peasants who were used to be demanding toward their families and to doing with their body and family anything they wanted.

In a world where only the opinion of the ignorant and macho man mattered, all those changes sounded like insults to manhood. In the *tendajo* or little market on the ranch, the men gathered to exchange ideas and opinions about the new family orientation; the men felt their pride was sorely wounded by the insolence of social workers who dared to tell the men "how to live their lives. Feeling offended by such daring made comments of the program's rejection very common. One of the most often heard comments was some variation of this one, "Those lazy old ladies (referring to the social workers), who have no other things to do and who know nothing about life should be taking better care of their families and let others live."

Meanwhile, in Ana's home, her family, and especially her parents, tried to digest what they heard from the talks about family orientation. Don Ira continued to profess the idea that women must obey the men, and Igna should continue producing children until her body would give up. He also said that if there was a time of shortage and crisis, there would soon come a time of abundance. The people of the world must suffer to deserve. He held the opinion that the revolutionary ideas that would change the status quo would be very difficult because these teachers and social workers just did not understand the needs of a man.

Mrs. Igna, tired of a life of scarcity and calamities, on the other hand, began to think deeply and often about the possibility of a new and different life. She was trying to convince Don Ira that he should explore some new options. One of those options was expressed by the question, "Why not space out the reproduction a little? At least we should wait until the family has more food and probably more money to buy the basics for living," Even though Igna dared to express her ideas, sometimes with firm resolve, she did not impress Don Ira. He just continued telling her, "You complain too much. Is there anything you need? There are enough beans and tortillas." He was right. There were always some rotten tortillas and beans with weevils for the family members. Meanwhile, in the lady's mind, the seeds of curiosity and hope for a different life were germinating, seeds planted by the new government programs. The day came when she had to see her doctor about some ailments that could not be cured with home remedies. Mrs. Igna had secretly saved a little money from Don Ira for contingencies. After asking and getting permission from her husband to see the doctor in the city, she rode the bus to the nearby town. The comadre had received instructions on helping the family prepare dinner for the rest of the children who had been left at home. On the first evening, the comadre came home, prepared a pan of greasy potatoes with beans and left, leaving Ana to serve dinner and wash dishes. Ana, at just eight years old, would be responsible to see that all was well, to organize the kitchen, and to put the rest of children to sleep.

THE PUNISHMENT

The next afternoon, the lady of the house returned. Mrs. Igna showed a face of remorse and guilt. "How was the trip?" asked Don Ira, looking into her face with disgust and distrust.

The lady lowered her head and said, "Well, so?"

"Why what happened?" said Don Ira.

Igna, without being able to hide her guilt, replied, "I didn't do anything wrong. I just wanted to get contraceptives." She had talked to the doctor about the size and economic status of family. The doctor had suggested that planning the size of the family was a decision made by the couple together. They should decide the number of children they were able to maintain. The doctor, before she left his office, had given her some contraceptives only to try while the couple talked about reaching a decision.

Don Ira, frowning, his forehead furrowed in great authority, added, "Those stupid doctors don't know anything of the needs of a man. Besides, who cares for the doctor's opinion if he won't support my kids?" Don Ira continued his sermon as if he were disciplining a ten-year-old boy. "If you continue with these nonsense ideas, God will punish you. You are denying his will."

The lady said nothing, just bowed her head in shame and guilt and looked down the floor as if she were receiving a well-deserved punishment for challenging the will of the lord of the house. Suddenly, Don Ira noticed a cut on Igna's knee. He asked, "What happened to your knee?" Doña Inga explained, with some regret, that she had fallen down exiting the bus due to nerves and had scraped her knees. Don Ira then reinforced his scolding by saying, "What did

I say? Worse things might happen if you followed through with your plans for contraception."

As a result of this scolding, nobody mentioned the subject again. A few days later, Igna began to experience nausea and mood changes. Ana, with her innocent curiosity, asked what was really happening. Igna worried that she was sick from something. No one could explain her symptoms, so Ana decided to ask Aunt Lolita what was going on.

Aunt Lolita knew everything about Ana's thinking. Lolita explained to Ana that sometimes when a woman becomes pregnant, they have some aches and pains. When Ana heard the word "pregnancy," she felt that a hole had been ripped in her stomach. With that news, her hope that things would improve and dreams of a better life were shattered. Any hope of a better life was as far away from Ana and her family as the horizon. Ana, at just eight years old, sadly watched the depressing environment fill with coldness. She was concerned about her malnourished siblings in their rotten clothes and heads full of lice. On more than one occasion, at sunset, the ladies would gather outside their homes to talk about their sorrows and complaints. They have said that lice were coming out of the *pinsion*, probably referring to depression.

EDUCATION AS PART
OF THE SOLUTION

When someone tells you that you can't, it's thought
to be the reflection of their own limitations, not yours.
Ana

As Ana watched her world continue to stagnate, she kept thinking that something had to be done to change the situation. One of her early ideas was to work hard so others did not complain about her laziness. Working hard, in Ana's mind, would leave her time to follow her dreams of change. She continued trying to be useful and help as much as possible in order to learn all that she could at home and in school. Ana would attend school in the morning, returning home to help with the chores assigned by her parents that would take her the rest of the day. Her duties still included bringing the water from the well for daily use, washing children's diapers, and bringing wood to start the fire. She also washed dishes, cleaned the beans, shelled the corn, and other duties as required. With her everyday chores, there was no time during the daylight hours to do the homework. At night, by the light of candles or an oil lamp, Ana would take out her books and paper to finish her homework and prepare for the following day's classes.

Before her evening studies could begin, she had to collect the *Hay* (paistle) to make her own bed on the floor. In the morning, Ana, sore and painful, would get up from the cold ground and pretend that all was well. The first task of the early hours was to bring water from the well to wash the hominy (*nixtamal*). By completing those tasks, she would ensure for herself her own breakfast because, according to the law of Don Ira, "If one did not work, one did not eat." After breakfast, Ana had to grind the corn to make the tortillas, sweep the patio, watch over the kids, and make her parents bed. With so many chores, Ana forgot that she was entitled to some time to be a kid. Dressed in a beggar's clothes as she usually was with her long hair that was sometimes full of bugs, she was worried about only one thing, "Is there any way to get out of this misery?"

In her small world which lacked affection and the most basic necessities, another question plagued her, "How was it possible that no one cared about the people who live in these depressing conditions?" The solution to rising above her poverty-controlled world that was beginning to gain power within her consciousness was education. The idea persisted no matter the obstacles that were placed in her way. For her, there were no dreams remotely close to Santa Claus, the Wise Men, or the Wizard of Oz. Such characters existed only in the books teachers provided her because even books were scarce at the ranch. Ana had no other distractions more dear to her than reading books by the light of the candles and from stargazing at night. When she became too tired to stay up, she would go to sleep in her assigned corner which had been allocated to her, like a baby animal's stall in a stable. Her parents slept peacefully in their bed of thick mattress. It was a bed supported by glass bottles, so nobody would climb up and play on the bed.

Ana was also responsible for making the bed, with the term "bed" only referring to the parents' bed. Besides making her parents' bed, she had to pick up the rags, which were the improvised beds for the other children who, in the parents' minds, did not deserve a decent bed. Among her other household duties were picking up the dirty clothes and emptying the chamber pot that her parents alone had the right to use. The children had to go outside to relieve themselves, no matter the temperature or the lateness of the hour. When she had picked up the house, Ana would sweep the floors and shake the dust from the tablecloth. Her final housekeeping chore saw Ana sprinkling water on the dirt floor to settle the dust. If during those activities, Ana would sometimes show opposition, she would be marked by her father's belt to show she had been disobedient. Nothing kept Ana from going to school. Her attendance showed the consistency and the strength of her drive and willpower.

DISCIPLINE AS PART OF
FAMILY TRAINING

As part of the progress of the new presidential reforms, the government decided to improve the roads of the nation and, at the ranch, to upgrade the *camino real*, "national highway." Improvements were needed to widen and properly surface the road of the camino real in order to serve the trucks that regularly make deliveries to the community. Without announcements, several trucks full of people wearing orange helmets rolled into the village. With them came men who would supervise the project. The supervisors organized a board at the school to inform the peasants about the work schedule. Project engineers informed the crowd that they would use gunpowder to plot holes, which would be very loud when workers set the charges off. The engineers knew that the blasting would arouse people's curiosity. The engineers wanted everyone to use extreme caution in getting too close to the construction area.

The next day, the big project began. From a safe distance, villagers could see men yelling to each other and hear the rumblings from the holes as well as seeing dust clouds caused by the explosions. Ana and her siblings curiously watched what was happening from a safe distance. One day, when Dad was away, their curiosity was greater than their fear. Ana and her brothers decided to move a bit closer to see the holes being blasted. It was a spectacle to see as giant rocks broke into small pieces or *desquebrajaban* as if they were sugar cubes. The children were mesmerized with the entertaining scene, so they did not realize that Don Ira had discovered them at their closer vista point. He descended on them like a cyclone with his angry wolf face and belt in hand. Ana and her brothers were literally paralyzed with fear.

Without any explanation whatsoever, Don Ira pushed them toward home and whipped them as if they were stubborn donkeys. When the troop arrived at their house, he continued to strike them until the children peed and pooped in their pants and he got tired. With belt in hand, he then forced the children to clean themselves. Since there was no explanation for the beating, only small curses and screams that sounded like hail or rain pouring from Don Ira's mouth, none of the children knew the reason for the beating. Days later, only the marks of the cintarazos remained on the children's bodies, and the memories of the punishment that none could explain remained etched in the children's memories for life.

There was never any explanation for the violent outbursts. Don Ira had no desire to overcomplicate his life with explanations. He had been born into and raised in a highly abusive environment. He had molded his family and world view in accordance to the scolding and physical punishment meted out by both his father and by other family members. He had little time to educate himself and barely completed third grade. He thought and bragged that was all the education he needed. Since "the animals," as he often described his family, did not see any need for lessons or explanations, why bother? Going to school was also sees as just a waste time. For Don Ira, it was more important to know how to work the land and care for the livestock. His intellect, shaped by his experience and lack of education, had not developed alternatives to his thinking in his family interactions, and therefore, he had no patience or skills to talking to his children. To correct negative behaviors, he only knew to hit them or punish them as he sometimes said he did with the animals he used when working his fields.

One day, with her father in a mellow mood, Ana gathered some courage as she recalled some past events and asked her father why he had so much hatred for his children. Accustomed to the verbal abuses and beatings, she hoped that her father, at some point, could explain the reasons for the beatings and his bad moods. Her question was a risk, but the only response she received was, "If you do not castigate the children, you don't care about them."

Ana did not find any logic in his explanation, which, as she later described, sounded like a mantra, and asked a new question, "Why can adults love others with hatred?" The situation created a conundrum. Ana walked from the room and wondered if the only two books Don Ira had ever read—*How One Triumphs in Life* and *Who Are You?*—had taught him anything no matter how much Don Ira boasted that he knew so much because he had read two books. He also prided himself with his selection of the titles; both were not written by a woman. After hearing his answer and thinking about it, Ana had no more to say. She did not insist on any further clarification and left the conversation where it landed. As she walked away, Ana knew she had to read more than two books to be able to understand her father's way of thinking.

READ TO GROW

That one who asks, arrives in Rome.
Popular Saying

Knowing that the only way to find the answer to her questions would be through learning, Ana thought that the best source of knowledge must be in the books or seeking answers from others with education and successful experiences. It was at that moment of decision that Ana dedicated herself to reading and to asking questions; she would put more attention to her surroundings. Ana began the next stage of her life's journey by reading all the books that she could buy or borrow. Each reading seemed to open a door to a world far different than the one she knew. She liked the writings in verse or prose found in stories, cartoons, and poems. Whenever she memorized a poem or a cartoon, Ana would always share it, so that she would never forget it. She mainly shared her readings with her parents although shared stories did not surprise them or impress them very much because her parents had their own stories.

Regardless of the opinions of her parents and ignoring their poor education, Ana shared her experiences with every book by introducing her newfound knowledge with phrases like these: "Would you like to hear something new I learned?" They did not answer her, but she would insist. "Well, I will tell you anyway!" She would begin reading or reciting a work, such as "How fresh is this morning, air enters through the nose, dogs bark, a child cries, and a plump and pretty girl is grinding corn on a stone."

Ana's parents did not really enjoy Ana's verse. "That is the reason why I don't like that you go to school" said Don Ira. "They teach you pure nonsense stupidities."

"Then show me something interesting," said Ana.

"You are crazy, can't you see that we have much to do?" said Mr. Ira. "Ana, stop being annoying and go to see if the pig laid an egg."

Ana replied, "They do not lay eggs but maybe women do. Grandfather said that women lay babies. Although I didn't think so because I've never seen them lay eggs. I have only seen women become so inflated like a balloon. Suddenly they deflate saying that the crane brought a baby."

With that, the lady would say, "Get out of here, damn girl. Go get yourself busy. Wash clothes, bring water from the creek, or sweep the patio."

But Ana was tired of working all day and answered back to her parents, "I don't want to be like you, ignorant. I'm going to go to school to study and make a different life for myself."

Her mother said, "Go to see if those books are going to feed you."

Ana said, "Just watch me. I'm sure they may help somehow."

In the mid-1970s, at the height of discussions like the one above, a missionary nun came to the ranch. She tried to educate the peasants through religion, so they could teach their children to live better in a quieter home. Ana, as always with her curiosity piqued, chatted with the nun and grew close to her. Ana, during one session, asked the missionary why people like to reproduce constantly without even having enough resources for their family's survival. The nun shook her head and said, "One day, when you grow up, you will understand."

Ana then replied, "But I want to know now, not later."

The missionary said, "Now you're just a girl. When you grow up, you will get married and you will have kids and a husband."

To this Ana replied, "No thanks. I will never marry and have a nag of a husband or, much less, many children."

At that, the nun attracted Mrs. Igna's attention. When Igna walked over, the missionary said, "It is very interesting what your daughter says."

Igna replied, "Yes! I do not know what is wrong with that girl's mind. We will see if one day she can focus or get some common sense."

"No," the nun relied with a great insight, "your daughter does not think like the rest of the children her age. She thinks in the future."

Ana quickly interjected, "I'd be like you, a messenger of God, when I get educated. I will teach people who don't know how to live."

The nun smiled benevolently and said softly, "Surely someday you will…" Later that day, she left.

As she had told the missionary, Mrs. Igna had a problem understanding Ana's behavior. She speculated that perhaps Ana hit her head as a toddler while running instead of walking on an uneven surface. When she fell, she hit her forehead on the ground and caused some damage. As a consequence of falling, Ana had done everything differently. She had learned to talk before she could walk. She began to walk without crawling, and instead of taking baby steps, she just stood up and ran. It never occurred to the lady that physical and mental abuse also makes the children change their behavior for better or for worse. Mrs. Igna's solution to the problem, recalled Ana, would be to give birth to another girl who would probably come out better than Ana. Igna began to work on her new project, a project easier said than done. She became pregnant in a blink of an eye. The odd aspect to this pregnancy was Igna's comment that she had so many boys by accident that she just wanted to have the girl of her dreams, a dream held since Ana was born. Ana could not understand her mother.

A few months after that conversation, Igna's pregnancy became quite noticeable, and Igna was sure she was pregnant with a baby girl based on the power of her wish. Another piece of evidence in Igna's favor was she was not as moody as she had been during her other pregnancies. As in many things, whether for good or bad or from one of those things just happening for a reason, one day brought a memorable but tragic event to the family. Don Ira, because he did not have enough people to help him, worked alone in the cornfield, his *milpa*. To get a donkey load of corn back to his house, he sent an acquaintance who was passing by to take the donkey to his home. The man went directly to Ira's home but, being in a hurry, did not unload the donkey. Mrs. Igna noticed that the donkey standing in the sun. The heavily loaded donkey appeared tired, so she tried to unload it herself. Big mistake! When she untied the load, she rested it on her belly, and the fetus could not handle weight and pressure. Almost immediately, Igna began to feel labor pains, and she looked for help, but it came too little too late! The lady suffered a miscarriage. To make matters worse, the baby was a normally developing girl who, according to Igna, would have been born if carried to term. Igna, in her sorrow, could not make the connection of how things happen for a reason or what that reason might have been.

PROLIFERATION TO AVOID
LOSING THE PRACTICE

A few months later, Igna was pregnant again, but at that time, she was already resigned to carry the baby to term. All the family planning brigades, the educational pamphlets, and the radio propaganda approaches of "small family lives better" had little effect on her. On the contrary, instead of stopping the increase in family size, the family planning program administered more fertilizer to increase the family's farm production. It made no difference to the family that the kids were rebellious, were always hungry, slept on the dirt floor, were covered in lice and parasites, and lived in a hostile environment. Nothing stopped Ana's parents from their task of having all the children that Igna's body could produce.

Months later, on the assigned day, the next baby was born, and as Igna suspected, it was another machito, a boy. After giving birth to another brown boy, the idea of having the blonde girl with blue eyes vanished. The only option left to her, as she understood or the scheme of things, was to accept what came. The baby was not white but looked exactly like his father said a family friend. Since the newborn was morenito, "brown," the child had more resistance to disease, did not get sick as easily, and if ill, recovered faster than the gueritos, the "whites." According to his mother, gueritos were more delicate. In the end, it did not matter to her—Igna's feelings were irrelevant—if a new born was a boy because boys were Don Ira's favorite.

Nearly two years later, the next baby was born, and that time the baby was white, a guerito, to the delight of his parents. The boy was born white or light-skinned, and that was the curious thing, the

49

baby came from the womb malnourished and very frail. His skin was as white as snow; at times, it was hard to know if his skin was yellow or pale or was only due to his natural whiteness. The baby had very black hair like a tuft of reeds on the left side of the head and small very black eyes. Igna was not too concerned about the baby being malnourished; she just knew he would feel better with her giving him her affection. She called him Chabela chegunda, referring to Queen Elizabeth II. Nonetheless, living at the very bottom of her fantasy was the long-held dream of the baby being girl. Consequently, Igna passed much of her time entertaining and caring for the new boy. That meant Ana was in charge of caring for the rest of the kids because with the newborn as the center of her world, Igna had no time for the others.

Even with the newest infant, the family picture was not yet complete. There were some spots to fill. Since the guerito did not develop as easily or as quickly as the other kids, the lady became concerned and decided to read the brochures on nutrition that the social workers and health educators left as part of the family planning programs. The brochures said mothers should start trying to feed the babies with foods other than milk as early as three months of age. They advised the parents to have the infant develop a taste for solid food and, eventually, learn to eat adult food. The lady, not fully understanding the advisories and not thinking the process through, took a bottle of milk, added a raw egg, and fed it to the baby. The next day, she noticed that the baby was getting some color, but it was an odd reddish color because he could not defecate. Not realizing that there was a problem, she was excited that, at last, the baby was "grabbing some color."

Another day went by, and the baby was not red anymore. Instead, he turned purple because he could not poop. The comadre and the other ladies of the village suggested remedies, such as enemas so that the baby boy could have a bowel movement. When the village remedies failed, the village women said that the solution was to pray and mourn. "Maybe he would die. What a shame as cute as he was," the ladies said. Four days after ingesting the milk and egg mixture, the baby would not stop crying. Ana asked the ladies if he needs to get checked by the doctor. When rebuffed, Ana continued, "Perhaps the doctor could do something to make him defecate." The ladies looked at Ana as if she had two heads and finally just dismissed her. "Go, girl, until you have something meaningful to say."

The next day, the baby was almost too weak to cry. Really worried, Igna left the village with her little ill baby to see the doctor. As usual, Ana was left in charge of the rest of the kids. That duty was good for Ana because, according to her mother, in addition to caring for the children, Ana must also learn how to cook. The lesson was very simple: Ana learns or the family starves to death. Ana's trials at preparing meals were short-lived because the mother returned the next day with the already cured guerito. The doctor had given him something that helped him defecate. The doctor further recommended that the lady take more attentive care of him since she nearly lost him by waiting to seek proper care. The doctor's orders or directions, however, were beyond the mother's comprehension. In her world, she believed that if one baby dies, the parents *replaces* the deceased child by another. However, in spite of the inappropriate care, the baby boy was saved, so the family continued the family tradition, and Don Ira's thought that his lineage would spread far and wide according to his idea of life.

THE REPRODUCTION
CONTINUES

Igna, not missing a beat, was again pregnant a few months following the incident with the youngest child. Don Ira said, "It is good. God gives children to those who deserve them." Ana, in an idea 180 degrees from that of her father, felt as if she and her siblings were sinking into a dead end and bottomless well of desolation and despair. How was it possible that someone could think of having more children in an environment so bleak and depressing? How could her parents see their life as being the ideal life? It was, at that moment, affirmed beyond all doubt, that Ana's parents had no idea of their children's suffering. Furthermore, they did not worry about their children's welfare because the cradle for the new born was ready year after year. Whenever they brought a new baby into the world, the previous one would, from that day forward, sleep on the floor and had to survive the floor's cold, hard dirt since life was not easy for anyone.

Ana was constantly trying to distract herself from her life's miserable scenario. She listened to songs for children and lullabies like the ones composed by popular singer of child songs, Don CriCri. Among her favorites were "Mrs. Duck" and the "Three Little Pigs." The latter said, "The little pigs are already in bed, many good-night kisses mother had given, and cozy and warm (*calientitos*), all in pajamas, in a while, the three will snore (*roncaran*)." Ironically, the songs only contrasted her world more deeply, increasing her sorrow. Ana and her siblings slept on the uneven, hard, and dusty floor on a broken, smelly mat covered with pieces of old, dirty blankets. The parents still slept in bed with a thick spring mattress, covered in blankets that, although smelly, were plush, warm, and much newer than the ones the children had. Nonetheless, the parents were oblivious of the misery in their children's lives. Even if they did know, it seemed they knew how to hide it quite well, never sleeping on the floor.

As life continued, the couple (*senores*) were continuing their task of having children. For the parents, there was no point of return to normality, as the social worker's family planning pamphlets told them, because the parents were already poor and ignorant and had to endure the rod as the condemned do, and life will go on as always. Harvests continued to grow even smaller as the drought continued. Sometimes, there was no water in the well and people would fight to get the last few drops of clean water to drink. For other needs, Ana had to bring the dirty water from the creek to boil. Almost daily, in order to survive, the ladies would fight for a bucket of clean water from village's well that no longer produced enough water for the village's needs. Ana, caught in this struggle, had to wake up before dawn, before the sun touched the eastern horizon with light, to bring a little water for the whole family to drink and was confronted or challenged by the older people who were trying to get some clean water too.

It was during that time of struggle that Ana began to feel ill. She did not know if it came from physical weakness or stress or both. She developed some white spots all over the body, and the white part of the eye turned yellow. Aunt Lolita tried to cure Ana with her usual folk remedies with no effect. Ana developed nausea and refused to eat beans with weevils that were the only thing the family had. Her parents were not too worried about Ana's not wanting to eat since it meant more food for the other family members and brought to mind the old saying, "Among fewer donkeys, there are more cobs." What really worried them was that she could not work as fast as she had before falling ill. That realization stirred the parents to action. They took Ana to the doctor for the first time in her life. After examining her, doctor said that Ana was very anemic and prescribed some pills. He recommended that she eat meat. When Ana heard this, she felt as if someone had thrown her a lifeline to keep her afloat. Red meat was what she wanted most, but having red meat was only a dream since the family ate meat only when someone at the ranch decided to kill a bull or shoot one that fell into the ravine or ditch and had been found by the villagers before the meat spoiled.

Fortunately, Ana overcame the anemia, and a few months later, Ana resumed her household duties. Just as Ana was able to get back on her feet, Mrs. Igna started with her aches, pains, and her bad moods. Ana recognized the signs immediately; her mother was pregnant again. Don Ira was very happy and said, "At last, there is good news. Probably this will bring us better luck." In time, the next son was born to the "happy" couple. This child was brown, *prietito*, but at least the baby was a boy, papa's little man. The concern came because the boy did not have anything under his arm, a phrase meaning physical features they expected a boy to have. Already fixed and fed for life. People reassured the parents that there was no reason to worry about the newborn since many boys were born with their fate hidden under the arm. Soon nature will make things right. While that discussion filled the lives of the village women, the lady still dreamed of having a girl. To make that dream more real in her eyes, she called the boy *mi negrita*, "my little brown girl." Many years later, he would truly surprise parents. He did not transform himself into a girl, but the "little woman" had other tendencies that the couple had never thought would happen to one of their children.

After rejoicing at the arrival the newborn son, it occurred to Ana's parents that food, clothing, and other basic necessities were in very short supply. And at that time of the season, Don Ira noticed that there was little work to do, and he was unable to provide for his family. In hopes of making a brighter future, at least a sustainable one, he left to find work outside the ranch. Unfortunately, he left the lady with a lot of little kids and almost nothing to eat. Although it was very common for Igna's face to express the hopeless of her life, when left alone to care for the family, the lady had a look of both sadness and desolation and much more worry than usual. She found no cheer from the village chatter because the gossips never missed an opportunity to spread malicious comments. They whispered among themselves yet always loud enough of others to hear that it did not matter that Igna gave Don Ira a bunch of kids, *chamacos*, he left her anyway. The final weight placed on Igna's shoulders came when she realized that their account or credit at the little convenience store, the *tiendita*, was running out. To keep everyone fed, Igna told Ana that they must eat a tortilla with a tomatillo salsa from the tomatillos she collected from the field while the other children had to settle for soup made of beans and tortilla pieces because times were so bad that even the hens would lay no eggs.

Eventually, Don Ira returned from his trip. He had managed to work a bit and save some money; however, after paying off the debt incurred during his absence at the convenience store (tiendita), he was left with little to survive. That event was a learning experience for Don Ira and Doña Igna. Since then, Ana's parents realized that they had a complicated life. Finally, they admitted to themselves that the small family lives better particularly in those times of crisis even though they had often denied it on many past discussions. However, rather than accept that the educators were right, Don Ira rationalized that "hunger is bad, but worse is the one who endures it." According to Don Ira's further rationale, "someone who complained about his state in life does so because he is a coward." Ana listened with caution because, if she or any other family member questioned those ideas, her parents would scold or punish the questioner.

Despite everything that was happening, Don Ira did not want to leave his lands as some people had suggested. People told him that the best thing to do was to go to the big city to find work. Old habits die hard, and traditions are hard to let go. Don Ira did not want to stop working his plot, which no longer produced even for the most basic needs, and the sparse rains could no longer help the sterile lands. Many families had already realized the futility and hopelessness of staying on the ranch and had left for the city. Those families went away, some with strong hopes and some with dim hopes, to seek a new life that would give them at least for the basics. The government, seeing so many people deserting the rural lands, did not know how to deal with so much emigration from the farms to the cities and implemented orientation programs. For the peasant, the government invented songs that made the rural residents think as "a farmer wept"; others tried to discourage them from moving to the city. The government was very aware that more people in the city made the crisis worst.

Don Ira got very thoughtful while listening to the song "A Farmer Wept." Before the song ended, tears of sadness welled from his eyes although he said that males don't cry. He began to think that he had to work for others, which was difficult for him to accept, having been self-employed for so many years. As the crisis at the ranch worsened, poor Don Ira gave serious consideration to the possibility of going to the city. Don Ira finally saw his eight children as they really were, sickly and malnourished. As that picture sharpened, he thought that the universe had conspired against him. Ana too continually studied the depressing situation, made more so by knowing that, for her father, the possibility of getting out of the abject poverty was very remote. As discussions on moving or staying were bandied about, suicidal thoughts crept into Ana's mind with her father's continuing failure to make the decision to move the family out of their misery. Continuing to live the ranch life was not worth living. Though suicidal thoughts often drifted into her consciousness, Ana had too much sense to dwell on such nonsense. She would force the negative vibes from her life by recalling her dream of success through education though sometimes she did think seriously of ending her life.

Ana reviewed different options available to her if she attempted suicide and analyzed the many possibilities if her attempt should fail. If the attempt were not successful, she would most likely be crippled, or even worse, she would be a burden to the family. Maybe not. No one gave a poop about her, so it did not matter what she thought or did. If her attempt succeeded, nobody would benefit from it. Wait! On the contrary, the family would think that as "fewer donkeys, more cobs" would come into play, and her siblings could eat the crumbs, which normally would fall to her plate.

The suicidal ideas vanished when she began praying for the Almighty to help the family by granting her the miracle of leaving that depressing place she called home. Not long after she began praying, her miracle was granted when, suddenly, someone arrived from the city. During long conversations, the visitor tried to convince Don

Ira that it was best for the family to go to the city. There, a man would find him a job in a factory. In a short time, having saved some money, he could pick up his wife and kids if they could survive the hunger and famine. Hearing that, Ana could not believe that her prayers had been answered and then knew that God had not abandoned her. When she arrived at the city, the first thing she would do was to go to the church to give thanks to the Lord.

During that period of uncertainty and stress, Ana suffered many bizarre dreams and sleep-killing nightmares. In a prominent one, she dreamed that she fell into a bottomless abyss and never touched the bottom; she just kept falling. In another vivid dream/nightmare, she dreamed that she was crossing a river; suddenly, slippery rocks caused her to fall into the swift, cold water. In a third very well-remembered dream, huge black dogs attacked her, and she had to destroy them by hacking them to pieces. When hope of a move to the city and a change in her life began to take root and bring hope to her life, the content of the dreams began to change. She had more control over the dreams' content. Since then, when she fell into the abyss, she could seize the grasses surrounding the well. And if she failed to grasp a hold, she would continue to sleep and woke up in the middle of the fall. As for the dogs, she would be prepared, so when they were nearby, she would cut into their head with a huge, very sharp pair of scissors or a giant knife. She could also control what felt like the flight of her soul. In that nightmare, it was as if her soul abandoned her during those nights of intense cold that reached to her bones and that nearly left her unconscious. Such cold caused her joint pains (rheumatic pain) during most of the winter.

A few weeks after the meetings with the visitor, the vague, shapeless idea of moving to the city struggled to life and took shape. Don Ira finally decided to find a job in the city, packed his meagre belongings, and left. Shortly thereafter, a letter for Mrs. Igna arrived from the city. Don Ira told her that relatives had found him work in a factory, and that he had found a place to live. The news could not have been better to Ana because the news represented a complete change in the household. At the very least, the lady would stop complaining about her destiny. Ana hoped that, in this new, yet unknown place, there would be food to eat. Ana envisioned no longer having to look at the hunger marking the faces of her brothers after the small portions they currently had to eat. She pictured a life much less cruel than the one she was living on the ranch that was full of poor, ignorant people. She entertained thoughts of no longer suffering from the bad vibes that made her sick just by being close to the people of the ranch. The new world just had to be more promising. At least the people in that distant and unknown place had plenty to eat. That was the new world that Ana imagined for the whole family.

After packing their *tiliches* (suitcases) with their few belongings, the family was ready and waiting for Don Ira to return and to take the family to the new place. The days of waiting seemed eternal, but finally, the happy day of their departure arrived. The first duty was to negotiate the lease of the small house Ira had built with his own hands and with so much sacrifice. Next, Don Ira said good-bye to his compadres and the people who would remain on the property, trying to survive with what others had cast aside on their journey to a better life. Ana, at the time, did not understand why it hurt so much for Don Ira to leave that sad and dry place. She saw nothing but the dried and dead crops, the greenery that promised food and money to spend at the little store was only a distant memory. What remained of the once bountiful orchards were only a few giant trees, such as walnuts. Looking back on that moment, she noted that the drought dried up more than just the lands. It had dried up the hopes and dreams of all the people as well. With one last look at his desolate home and his once fertile fields, Don Ira made a promise to himself that one day he would return to have his own piece of land full of trees.

THE NOSTALGIA OF DEPARTING

Ana and her family were preparing to leave the only home most of the family had ever known. They were leaving with mixed feelings that hung like a black cloud over the family because the family knew they would never return. Even Ana, who so badly wanted to leave the ranch behind, could not help feeling nostalgic. She had so many good and bad memories, memories that crowded her mind and played like a dramatic film in the cinema. She recalled the calamities and the hardships, and in between these dark moments, the few good memories. Ana, standing in the street ready to depart, wondered how she would ever forget the first house that she saw in her first moments of life. She wondered if she would ever forget the patio which divided the house into sleeping and the kitchen sections, that great covered patio by the bower that Ana had swept with a broom made of green thickets, the broom that filled her hands with calluses. She recalled the huerta, the garden that was once so fertile with its trees heavy with pomegranates, peaches, and apples. She thought of the nearby plot that once gave corn and zucchini for soup in the fertile times; the plot now so barren, so sterile. She recalled, almost wistfully, another plot which had once been so productive, a plot where Ana and her siblings had planted grain under the blazing sun. Finally, she recalled the little stream, just a creek really, that provided water to drink, water to wash the family's clothes, and water to quench the thirst of their animals.

As she trudged down the road to the bus, Ana could not forget the fresh mornings and the warmth of the summer days. She thought too of the winter mornings when the cold would wrap its icy fingers around her bones on those frigid, wet winter days that made her ill with rheumatism and made her cry. As those varied memories flooded her thoughts, she compared the days of bitter cold and biting winds with the days of warm summer rains that felt so good. She remembered, with mixed feelings, the bucket of nixtamal, the cooked corn that she had to grind with the hand mill. Intermingled with these thoughts of the life she was leaving behind that whirled in her head in great confusion like debris in a cyclone was the question, How in the world were people able to think that this peasants' way of life was accepted by the people of the ranch without protest? How did the peasants accept a lifestyle in which nobody talked about love, happiness, or the fantasy/dream of a different world? This world from which she was walking away one step at a time was the ranch of El Saucito (The Willow) where only lamentations and sorrows prevailed.

THE WILLOW AND
THE LAMENTS

The Willow was the name of the village in which Ana's family and thirteen other families, each with its own character, lived and worked. The weeping willow families, as Ana thought of them, lived inside that small ranch and often cried, complained, and lamented their tragedies; yet somehow, they endured. On the south side of the ranch, Doña Andite lived with her sons, Tony and Kiko. Nobody ever saw her husband. People thought she was a widow. The younger son, Tony, supported the family because Kiko, the oldest, had lost his mind, or so the people said. Kiko never worked; he just walked throughout the ranch, mumbling or rambling as if his mind were in another world. Neighbors said that a bad woman had used witchcraft that had left him crazy. No one thought that Kiko might be suffering from a type of mental illness rather than from a witch's spells. That small family lived with their problem and prayed to relieve their sorrows.

The second family belonged Neto and Pancracia, cousins of Doña Andite's family. They had four living children, but people gossiped that the lady had lost several children because of her practicing witchcraft. The evil tongues whispered that Pancra practiced witchcraft to get rid of any one whom she did not like; they further said that during the night of the full moon, she would wear ointments that made her, as well as her broom, invisible. Since she could not see with her own blind eyes, she took sight from cats on the nights of the full moon and saw better at night in order to spy more successfully on those whom she would cast a spell on. Pancra knew how to bring down owls that would help her clearly identify those on whom she worked her witchcraft on. Her children, however, were not vilified as their mother was. Tony learned to play the accordion and played at the small parties held on the ranch. His brother, Nacho, helped him by playing guitar. The two rehearsed every evening after work. When the people on the ranch heard the brothers practicing, everybody suspected there was a party coming. Lupe, her daughter, helped Pancra with the housework, and the smallest child was the goat herder. The youngest one was pretty wild. Aside from using obscene vocabulary when talking with others, he was very rude to his classmates and a real headache for his teachers. On one occasion, he stole the money that the students were giving the teacher for Mother's Day. He would constantly fight with his classmates, be they boys or girls. to scare to the girls, he would expose himself. No one knew why he was so evil.

Felix was patriarch of the third family, and he was quite wealthy. people called him the rich man of the ranch. People speculated that Felix had found a pot filled with gold coins. People, for many years, have told stories in these outposts of civilization of peasants who, through luck or by accident, were able to find treasures that rich people (usually farmers and landowners) had buried during the war against the revolutionaries in the early 1900s. With the money from the treasure, Felix had managed to open the tendajo, the convenience store. He also bought fine cattle and had a large family. He entertained the family with the tendajo and taught them the value of money. Felix was in charge of buying and caring for their cattle. He only one bought and bred Charolais cattle as well as bringing in pedigree bulls for breeding and Hereford steer for beef. However, with all his wealth, people could not explain his having a wife as ugly and skinny as she was. The gossips also found it most curious that the couple had a dozen children!

Felix always wore white nose caps. People said that he had a rare disease caught while unearthing the treasure because he had not had time to shield his nose from gases or poison at the site of the treasure trove, and as a result, he had damaged his respiratory system. From that point on, he would have to use medicine for the rest of his life. Interestingly enough, that had not prevented him from having a dozen kids with Petra, his wife. Petra, as mentioned, was a skinny and rough woman who never wore makeup, always dressed in rags, and went barefoot everywhere. People never understood her behavior or had an explanation for her dress. Among themselves, other townspeople asked of Felix, why, being a rich man, he could not have found someone better since men with money always chose from the most beautiful women on the ranch and always dressed them elegantly.

Felix did not care what people said or thought; the couple had made a great family. Lela was the oldest, as colorless and thin as her parents, but the men were besieging her because she is the eldest daughter of Don Felix. However, for Felix, no man was worthy of having Lela. The result of her father's protectiveness from questionable suitors was her being kidnapped by one of her suitors. Mina was not very graceful. She was born with *virolo* eyes, which is more commonly called cross-eyed. She was also skinny and her face was heavily pockmarked. She was easygoing and not at all presumptuous. She was very religious and liked to invite the kids from other families to walk with the rain saint, San Isidro. When she walked, she would adorn a chair with the photograph of the holy saint and would walk into the different fields of corn or *solar*, then sing, "Lord San Isidro, revered holy saint, your rain has given a nice planted...," while followed closely by a group of children. Curiously, when the ritual ended, people began to feel the rain. It rained so hard that, by the time all children returned home, the storm was in full swing, and everyone was soaked.

Lencho was the tendajo attendant. As such, he just knew how to make money. In reality, he did not know anything else but working in his father's store. As the pompous clerk, he tried to buy favors from the girls in the ranch. He had no social skills, and as such, he could not charm anyone with his personal appeal. Besides his lack of social skills, he was described as ugly and would become tongue-tied during social situations because he stuttered. His brother Filo was also a stutterer and had a club foot, or what people in the village called foot throw. Whenever he walked, he would throw his foot to the right before taking the next step. Chui and Elena were the most normal. They were the scholars of the family. Gulf, who also stuttered, was good at school. Pita, Crista, Chayo, and the others had much to boast about since they were very small girls and were the daughters of Don Félix. Since Félix bragged and wanted his family to be a model family, people kept an eye on them through the race's gossip hotline. The tongue waggers said that although he was rich, he did not escape having children with defects. The rural people believed there can be no "beauty without defect, nor ugly without grace." The people also said that it was "easier for a camel to pass through the eye of a needle than for a rich man to enter into the kingdom of heaven." Were they jealous of Don Félix and his family? It seemed so.

Another family was that of Bunio and Soco's, two Solteros, single brothers, who had left the ranch too spend their youth working since they felt obligated to care for their mother, who was suffering from an incurable disease. They were quiet and submissive. They were among the very poor and never went to school. Their world consisted only of work, eating, sleeping, and caring of their ailing mother. The poor lady lived in nearly constant pain. Everyone knew of her sufferings because all the residents of the ranch could hear her moans at all hours of the day and night. Some people said that her bones and joints hurt as if they were burning her on the inside. The hut where she slept smelled horribly, the smell carried even on the nearby street. Neighbors said that the smell came from the remedies that the curandero applied to her. No one really knew the reason for her illness, but the superstitious people muttered that she was being punished for some unknown reason since even the best healers could not cure her. The ranch's children prayed that someday she would stop suffering. However, the old woman suffered her illness until God, taking pity on her, freed her from her pain and called her to heaven. After her death, Soco and Bunio, having only memories of her moans, lived their lives in abject poverty and desolation. They felt that they must pray daily so that they would not suffer the same fate as their mother.

The ranch's "almost family" belonged to Uncle Tolo's and his son, Beto. They lived alone, but people knew that many years ago, Uncle Tolo had once been married. Since he did not like to work,

Tolo sought a bride who would support him. It was said that he as young man was handsome or, at least, had a good presence. He told those who would listen that he was a descendant of Spanish nobles. He described himself as a caballero. He first wooed a woman named Keita, who was not very beautiful, but she refused to support him. Finally, with luck, he found a woman who accepted the deal to support him. Like Keita, she was not very beautiful. Those who knew Tolo's wife said that she was very *luchona*, a very hard worker. Aside from attending her husband, she made tortillas to sell to other people and took in washing and laundry for the neighbors to earn some income. The family, like most others in the village, raised chickens and turkeys, sold eggs, chicks, and *coconitos* to those who would buy them. At one point in their relationship, she gave Tío Tolo a child, so he could be entertained while he sat on his patio while his wife was off working. Their son, Beto, inherited his father's laziness but without his parents' grace or his father's looks. Both men relied on *pobrecilla*, the poor lady, to support them. Beto was slow in speech and motion, so to speak, and people often wondered if he was just born slow or if he was just plain lazy.

Unexpectedly, Tío Tolo's wife died shortly after falling ill. People said that she probably had an illness in her lungs, probably pneumonia, from working so hard for two lazy men. With her passing, they were then, essentially, two homeless men delivered unto the good grace of God. Neither of them knew anything about keeping a house or cooking, and since neither wanted to do anything, they would beg food from residents of the ranch when hunger overtook them. Most of the people became accustomed to seeing them usually visiting neighbors at lunch time or during the dinner hour. Sometimes they were lucky, and they stuffed themselves, and more than once, they developed indigestion, *se empachaban*.

They lived for many years as beggars. Villagers called the two useless and said as they shook their heads that Tío Tolo had become as *feito*, "ugly," as his son. No one would think about marriage for either one or even suggest it. One day, Tío Tolo became ill with "an old ache," as he said. Those neighbors who felt pity for him visited him. They wished to see what they could do for him. Unfortunately, the evil illness was already very advanced. He was raving. Between yelling and vomiting, he called on people to not let him die because he wanted to continue living, to keep eating. Even with all his sorrows and ravings, Uncle Tolo suffered with a very strong will to live, even though it was through the charity of others. Finally, Uncle Tolo died, leaving his son Beto helpless and without any tools or skills to survive on his own. Beto continued begging for favors and food from residents and died a few months later without warning "Water goes, a common expression." People grumbled that his father had sympathized with his son and had brought Beto to him to the spot where the father was spending eternity, or as the people said, "Only God knows where."

The unique bachelor of the ranch was Don Delfi. No one knew why he chose to live alone. When someone dared to ask why, he always gave different reasons or different stories. One of them, the most common, was that women made him sick since they were very filthy. Other gossips said that he was very stingy or disliked men and women. He spent most of his time in his garden, where he tended all kinds of fruit trees that provided for his living. Rarely would someone visit him. Sometimes, just to have some contact with the others, he would throw apples at children who passed by to draw a little attention. Delfi had decided to be a family of himself.

Vito and Pablito (Paul) was another household. They were a very unique couple. Vito was barely four feet tall while Pablito, her husband, was more than six feet tall. Vito had never learned to read and write but talked more than a crazy *cacatua*, a frightened parrot. She loved to gossip and lived to visit neighbors and talk about them as if she were "the newspaper of alarm" on the ranch. No one knew how she had time to be a housewife to Pablito and give birth to eight children. They even wondered how she had ever understood Pablito's proposal. Pablito, like his wife, was illiterate and hardly spoke to anyone. When he talked to someone, he would talk very slowly. Pablito would also walk slowly but with a long stride. Vito said that although she was chubby and had the waist of a hen, she had not always been so chubby. She blamed Pablito for having made her chubby by having so many children! Among their eight children, their two older daughters excelled, which surely helped to support the family.

Chuya was the oldest and helped Vito with the other children. However, when she reached adulthood, she fled to the city to work as a maid to help support the house. Eventually, she married and started her own family. By then, the next sibling was ready to work, to continue the fight for the survival at home. She too grew to adulthood. At that point, it was her turn to move away to earn money for the house. When the second daughter married, there was another in training and ready to help at home. Lupe, daughter number three, was the next on the list. Like her sisters, she dedicated herself to being a maid, but she was even more noble. By more noble, people mean that she became the heroine of the family because she not only supported her parents but also assumed the responsibility of caring for the two younger kids whom she tried so hard to guide from the family legacy of ignorance.

Lupe wanted to keep these younger siblings from suffering the family legacy of deprivation and a life of hard, physical work. She wanted her two brothers, May and Hetor, to study and become teachers. While the youngest child, Mary, would become a *secretaria*, "secretary." Lupe became their sponsor, endured many personal sacrifices, and pushed them to study hard to eventually pay back the family and herself for their studies. Unfortunately, their innate ability, or lack of it, did not help them travel on the road to success. It did not matter how much support Mary and the boys had, they could not keep up with the work because the books were too difficult for them. The boys never could graduate as teachers. Mary too was not able to complete her career training as a secretary. She could not remember the shorthand symbols and was a very slow typist. People said nothing else could be expected from children coming from two illiterate parents.

Another peculiar family was the family of Don Bucho. It was a family that rarely mingled with anyone. People only saw them when attending an event at the ranch or when they were on the bus as journeying passengers to the nearest town. To protect his family, Don Bucho had surrounded his solar, "parcel," with *nopales* (cactus) as protection. With such a prickly barrier, no one approached his daughters or tried to bother him. No one knew if he had a wife. And since he was the only one who traveled to the village and the store to pick up what the family needed, his life was a mystery. No one knew what happened inside of the *nopalera*; life on Don Bucho's lands was a mystery, and no one tried to befriend him.

Cleo and Conra were the names of the tenth family. Although their names were crossed—his name was derived from Cleopatra while wife's name was derived from a man's name, Conrad—they only wanted to be happy in their own world. He was skinny and *chaparrito*, "shorter," while she was *mas chaparrita*, even shorter and skinnier than he was. The men of the ranch gossiped that Cleo fathered only tiny girls, the only children they could have for being chaparritos, hobbits. The family had seven girls and a gingerbread boy, also a chaparrito. The oldest child was a tiny, skinny girl. Her neglectful mother took her out in the cold air while the house was very hot, and the impact of the cold air had caused one eye look off to the side (strabismus and amblyopia or lazy eye), so the poor girl saw with a wandering eye, of which she was much ashamed. The next child was the little boy who became a spoiled a brat. The parents cared for him as if he were made of gold since he was the only boy they would have. He also was chaparrito and had a mild learning disability. The second girl was very cute; she was like a little, very blonde doll (*curiosita blanquita*). No matter how pampered, she sometimes came to class with lice in her hair, which she tried to hide with the glitter her mother sprinkled on her head. She alone worked hard to get good grades. Next to be born was Maru. The poor thing was born browner than the others; therefore, the mother made her feel less of a person than her brother and sisters. After Maru came Paquita. Maru's younger sibling was very pale, as pale as a plastic doll. Maru, in time, fell ill with anemia when her mother failed to feed or care for her properly as her mother did for the other children, simply for being brown. Conra did not put much effort into curing Maru because Conra was very pregnant with another. Instead, Conra only provided Maru with leftovers and table scraps for nourishment. No one else in the family seemed to care that the poor thing was consumed slowly unto death by her illness. Soon Maru was yellow and just lay limply on her small bed. Conra too had to stay in bed because the day of delivery was nearing, and she was very fragile. One morning, from her small bed, Maru did not awaken. Her tired body had quietly, simply given up. Interestingly enough, her mother, Conra, gave birth the next day to another girl whom she named Maru. "In my recently deceased daughter's honor," she said. Conra said that life and God had provided a spare, just the way chickens are replaced. The new baby looked very similar to the one who had just passed away. By that time, Conra and Cleo would care for the newborn even though she was brown. Caring for this newborn properly was meant to be by divine decree since the newborn was so like the child who had so recently perished.

Family number 11 was the family of Beto and Rey. The lady of the house was called Rey. Beto was the eldest son of Don Greg. Although his father was hard working, Beto was not as smart or as industrious as his father. The only thing Beto inherited from his father was a taste for making children. Beto, like his father, had many little kids, which the gossipy people said were produced with the help of one or more volunteers. Rey had no close family in the region, or at least nobody knew her relatives. She said she was Christian, a.k.a. a sister. She said that brothers helped with food, money and clothing, so she did not worry if she continued giving birth to children left and right. The oldest daughters were Elvia and Nicky; they looked like twins but were born almost a year apart. The two were in charge of caring for the children until the sisters were mature enough to go to the city to work as servants or laborers. The succeeding children were Geno, Blas and Cesar. They were feitos, both ugly and evil. They were wild and had no education or manners. They were goat herders and did not like the school, preferring to spend time with their flocks.

Beto, the father of the children, was not ugly. As a result, the people grumbled that the kids were born ugly because someone had eaten his groceries (meaning he had not fathered those kids). However, when he heard these comments, poor, shy Beto was not angry and only blushed bright red. When money ran short and Beto could not provide enough money for the family, Rey would leave home. Before each leave-taking, Rey would be heard taking a bath. After which, she dressed in her best clothes, put on makeup, and wore perfume. She walked out to the road where passing truckers travelled, and with no money in her purse, she called for a ride. The truckers would stop and drive her to the nearest town. The next day, Rey would return well supplied with several bags of food and other basic items.

When she would talk with the neighbors of her adventures, she said, "Thanks to God who never deprived me anything," and push her chest up, breasts out, and then straighten here back to accentuate her butt. After her trips to town, the days would pass, and she would be pregnant again. One time, she gave birth to twins (*cuates*). The girl was born a brunette like Rey, but the boy had hazel eyes and fair skin. The neighbors, when they saw the twins, said that Rey had made a good choice of the one who had paid for the favor. Poor Beto, when he heard the hurtful comments of others, only blushed a deeper red, bowed his head, and walked on. Rey continued her work until she completed the dozen. With help or without help, Beto could not get a break at all. The ugly boys did not change, and later, they left to continue their job in the big city. One of the daughters became an exhibitionist who would be found making out as bride and groom in some spots of the ranch. Another daughter left, just disappeared. People said that she became pregnant and married in some faraway place.

Family number 12 was the Herrera clan that lived far from the rest of the people. They were really three families in one who lived very near each other. The mother of all of them, the matriarch, was an elderly lady who looked very different from the rest of the neighbors. Gina was her name. She had long black hair and very fair white skin, very different from others. Gina had very delicate features to go with her fair complexion; she looked and acted like no other residents of the ranch. They said she probably had Spanish blood. Though she knew her spells and potions, she was very different from the witch Pancra on the south side of the ranch. If truth be told, she did not mix with the riffraff of the ranch.

People whispered among themselves that she was a white witch. She was also the midwife, attending to some deliveries for the women from the ranch. Tella and the Guera were her youngest daughters; they were very nice, and no one dared to disrespect them. The locals said that the mother could practice witchcraft on anyone who dared speak ill of her daughters. At home, there were mostly adults who worked hard. Each of the families had garden plots that produced bountiful harvests. The Herreras also had many cows and were very protective of their livestock and lands. If someone was daring enough to trespass, the Herrera guns were at the ready. No one dared to mess with their animals, plots, or the sisters.

Family number 13 was Tita's family. Tita was the healer of the ranch. She had three children, Mago, Tota, and Nana. Tita had been widowed at a very young age. She had three very young children to raise. However, she cared for her family through her skills at several trades. She was the healer of the ranch, knew how to make griddles, and made tortillas for the ladies who paid for them. Most importantly, next to her role as a healer, Tita wrote letters for the illiterate who wanted to communicate with their families. It was with great sacrifice that she raised her three children. When Mago grew up, he was assigned a parcel of land, so he could work to support his sisters and his mother Tita. When Tota and Nana came of age and moved to the city to work as maids in wealthy houses, they contributed to paying the expenses of the house. After working for several years, Tota and Nana married and formed their own families. In time, Mago found a girl and brought his bride to live with him at his mother's home.

THE FAMILY MODEL

The family of Don Ira and Doña Igna, introduced earlier, were a couple with a long history of love for tragi-comedy, but more on that later. They also had a large family beginning shortly after their wedding day. Ana was the daughter they had never expected, even in their wildest dreams. She was born in midsummer with the sun as her star and planet regent and the element of fire as the basis of her life. She opened her eyes as soon as she was born, a feature not very common in those days. Apart from opening the eyes, she also seemed to carefully study everyone who approached her cradle. To make life at home more complicated for her parents, she began to speak before she could walk. She never crawled but sat up instead. Sometime later, but not too much later, she stood up, began to walk, and then to run. Regardless of how many times she fell on that uneven and cobbled floor, she would continue running.

Ana carefully observed the actions and interactions of those around her. It was as if she wanted to understand the world as reflected by anyone who entered her world. When something totally rare or new happened in her experiential world, she did not hesitate to ask and scrutinize the smallest detail. She wondered what would have happened to Kiko loco, whether Pancra was really a witch, or why Pancra's son, Bocho, was so evil that everyone in the ranch was afraid of him. Another question that puzzled Ana for many years was the reason for the painful disease of Soco and Bunio's mother. She even wondered at the contrast of the good luck of Felix, the wealthy, with the bad luck and poverty of others on the ranch. A corollary to her primary question was if he actually did find a treasure. Ana asked her parents how it was possible that only a few meters away from Felix lived Tío Tolo and his son Beto, who never had food to eat, never worked, or did anything with their lives. She was curious about Delphi's never marrying or forming a family, and what was the mystery of living alone. She wanted to know why Vito, who spoke as much as a cacatua, was illiterate, did not work, and had eight children. What was the mystery locked in the family of Don Bucho? Ana even noted at a very early age that the Herrera families did not mingle with anyone, but nevertheless, people respected them and wondered why. She looked carefully—perhaps it was better described as staring—at Senora Gina, the white witch, and asked if people called her that because she looked different from the rest of the ladies. She even voiced aloud questions related to Tia Tita. What really happened to her husband? What was the reason for her being such a luchona, a hard worker? Why was she always walking about the village with a look of sadness and desolation on her face?

Ana's parents were becoming overwhelmed by her questions and thoughts. Her parents, Don Ira and Doña Igna, had no patience or answers to satisfy her growing curiosity. To make the situation worse for Ana, her parents would punish her whenever she asked something that did not seem normal for a child her age. The parents' simple solution—punishment. It was their way of not complicating their life. Since she did not meet the characteristics that they expected in their offspring, they used her dynamism by putting her to work as a maid to see if she would change. The purpose of her punishment, at least partially, was to break her ego by lowering her self-esteem and by ridiculing her behavior. Apart from forcing her to do adult work and ensuring she avoided contact with the neighborhood children, her parents hoped she would not have any more ideas like the ones she already had. In addition to household duties and the ridicule was very limited play with any kind of games, toys, and the bestowing of the usual privileges of any girl her age. The final mode of correction employed by her parents was limiting both the type and quantity of food she received and by making her sleep on the floor. Those corrections were reinforced by beating her constantly. That latter action left bruises on her legs, known as marks of shame, which classmates teased her about them. What Ana's parents never imagined was that she had been born with a self-determination that was uncommon in those days. For Ana, no obstacle would minimize her will to live and explore the world both within her village and the much wider world beyond the village's fences. Those who met Ana later in her life would say that Ana's determination in those very difficult times could be described by the expression, "That which doesn't kill you makes you stronger." With her courage, anger, curiosity, and ambition, Ana would grow until the day she had the strength, knowledge, and experience to break the chains that tied her to her family and move on to the world she knew was there.

The second son of Don Ira and Doña Igna was the boy of their eyes. He was born as they had wished their son should be, a boy with fair skin and curly hair, a trait from his mother's family. They could not ask for more from life! There was one a tiny problem; he was very sensitive to the sun. Every time he was exposed to the blazing summer sun, he would develop nosebleeds. When that happened, they would send Ana to finish seeding the corn field. The family's pride was soon reduced to shame and pity at that child's condition rather than inciting punishment the parents usually brought down on Ana. Curiously, Ana's head also hurt, but she would recover more easily. Finally, the chino, as they called him, grew up and became the playboy of the neighborhood because Don Ira and Doña Igna allowed him free rein throughout his formative years. People who knew him began calling him a rooster and conqueror. He boasted that he had knocked up more than one girl. He was so vain that he thought he was untouchable. However, his vanity was given a flash of reality as he was getting ready to marry. He became very ill and thought he would die from someone having cast a spell on him. He consulted a doctor and a white witch to cleanse his spirit and thereby cure him. While lying on his sickbed, his conscience may have pricked him, and in his bitterness and fear, he predicted Ana would have a baby out of wedlock or become pregnant before her marriage. However, she did not have a boyfriend and was too busy going to school and working to have such a consequence. Eventually, the young man recovered, and with the passing of time, the law of karma visited his life and family. Twenty years after his so-called predictions, his precious daughter, a seventeen-year-old, whom he saw as his pride and joy fulfilled his prophecy when she had a child, fathered by the local teacher. When word spread of the liaison, she admitted the teacher was close, and she did not want to look any farther for a suitable lover and father.

The next child was the white guero like Chino, Don Ira and Doña Igna doted on him because he had been born a weakling. They named him Angel because they thought he was a miracle baby since Igna had not aborted him due to a fright sickness. The fright sickness was caused by Igna's brother coming to her in the middle of the night, bleeding from a stab wound he had suffered in a fight. That was what almost caused Igna to miscarry the guero. The weakling's description resulted from the baby's being listless and sickly. He did not develop as the parents expected. He was very unlike Ana. During his first few months of life, according to Doña Igna, he almost died, but was saved by a magic healer, who gave him his life back. The boy's recovery took a long time. During his recovery, it was difficult for him to turn over in his crib, and he even confused the poop of his diaper with food and ate it when his mother took too long to change him. What followed between missteps and a lack of character evident throughout his life, he grew up, fell in and out of love with free women like him. As he matured into adulthood, he drank constantly to forget who he was and to solve his many problems.

The fourth child was Sam, the one called the replacement. He was almost a year younger than the guero because Igna had conceived him thinking that if guero did not survive, they had their replacement ready to go. However, the guero survived, and the parents despised Sam, who did not understand the lack of care and affection he received, the opposite of the care given to the guero. Unconsciously, he developed the idea that he would survive no matter what others said or thought. He did not give a *cumin*, about others' opinions. As a baby, he would finish his bottle and take the bottle from the guero to satiate his hunger. When he could walk, he escaped to Tita's house to ask for a taco, which was more filling than the tacos given him by Igna. Don Ira pushed him to work harder than the guero because he, though skinny and malnourished, was stronger and was not as sickly and *quejambroso*, "whining," like guero. The result of that treatment was Sam's caring little for education. Sam was never ashamed of showing his report card full of red fives. He said that the red fives were an ornament for his card, and Don Ira's scolding did not bother him. When he became an adult, he always said that he was neutral and that he knew that was his life. After his thirty-fifth birthday, he started to get grey hair and thought it was time to find a woman to form what he called a happy family.

The next son of Don Ira and Igna was Tuito. It seemed that they had made him with hot pepper, the *chili piquin*, since baby Tuito was a real headache. He cried day and night for the slightest reason. He slammed his crib against the wall until he fell to the ground and then began to cry at the door until someone would rescue him. If he was angry or upset about someone or something, he would throw a massive temper tantrum, crawling toward the nearest wall, and banging his head against it. If the wall was far away from where he was sitting, he would simply drop his head to the ground and bang it on the floor in protest. On one occasion when his mother handed him to Ana to hold, he threw a temper tantrum. He twisted like a worm, and Ana lost her grip on him. The little boy slipped from Ana's arms and fell into the ashes and coals. His mother punished Ana, and *then* made sure that el Tuito was not burned. Luckily, he did not fall on hot embers, and nothing happened to the child. To take away the anger from the rebellious child, the family took him to see San Francisco de Asís, St. Francis of Assisi. The visit calmed him down a little as his parents hoped the visit would. Following the visit, beatings and scolding controlled him until Don Ira got tired. Unfortunately, another crisis of adolescence revitalized his rebelliousness. At that time, Don Ira, reverting to some earlier thoughts, called on Ana to come to the rescue. Between conversations with her and shame resulting from his activities, he gradually left the path of bad behavior on which he had been walking. The final steps on his path of violent, emotional outbursts, which were then few and far between, came with his engagement and wedding day. That was, he said, in thanks to a life that a good woman brought to him when she touched his heart. The love and gentle affection was probably what he was searching for and needed but did not find in his previous years. His marriage removed him from the risk of repeating the chain of rebellion and abuse.

Poncho was the next morenito in the family, who, by luck or circumstance, was not as rebellious as his older brother. By the time of Poncho's arrival, Don Ira was tired of beating the children. Consequently, Poncho did not receive the treatment that his older siblings endured. He did not feel the belt marks on his skin, and although genetics are hard to hide, he therefore would develop another vision of life. He liked to sing, so they allowed him to sing like a bird on the village streets when he was only five years old. That treatment and his gift for music made him think he was special; "enlightened" was the word he later used. His steps led him toward the kindergarten a few blocks from home, and that was the beginning of his good fortune. Outside the school, Poncho sang for the director of the kindergarten, a concert that the director found enchanting and piqued her curiosity. A few days later, when her schedule permitted, the director visited Poncho's parents and asked their permission to allow the child to attend the first year of kindergarten. No financial hardship, she quickly added to the parents' concerns; the director would take care of all expenses and fees. Poncho, as a result of his gifts and his scholarship, was the only family member to attend kindergarten, which helped him to further develop his intellectual and musical skills. He earned first-place scores in elementary school, and as a prize or reward, he traveled to several important states in the country. He also had the privilege of his parents attending his graduations since not all his brothers had that opportunity. He eventually completed his college degree, found a wife, married, and founded a family, fathering two children whom he loved and described as the little enlightened.

Key was the next in the family of eight boys. On the day he was born, he was as white as milk with a tuft of reeds or grey hairs and eyes as black as a moonless night. Doña Igna was mesmerized with their newborn because, apart from being *blanquito*, he was very quiet. Even his crying was calm. Once he became very sick because Igna made him eat a raw egg in the bottle of milk, which caused him to become extremely constipated. Poor boy, he almost died of indigestion, but he escaped through faith and proper care. After a few years, he forgot—if he ever knew—who gave him the food that made him sick nearly unto death. During his preschool years, Igna would forget to feed him, and he would pull her skirt reminding her that he had not been fed. When he grew up, it would appear ironic that he graduated in communications. However, when the family grew up and scattered, he stayed to live free in the house that other family members had built and then bought another house to rent. He did not marry.

Huicho was the next in the string of little kids. He was born in a time of crisis, the great drought. There was no rain, so there was no water. The land became sterile and unproductive from poor farming practices and a lack of water. That was not the case with the ladies of the ranch. To make matters worse, Huicho's parents were already tired from everything and everyone. The poor kid was morenito, and his mother did not care much about another morenito. Inga, called the poor Huicho, *mi negrita*, "my black," for being the dark morenito in the family. Igna paid little attention to him or to his needs. On one occasion, Igna did not want to wake up in the middle of the night to give him pats on the back in order to burp him after feeding him, and he almost died of indigestion. The good news was that she had Ana in reserve. She woke Ana up at three in the morning to care for the child. Ana, still very sleepy, took the baby in her arms. Seeing his face in the vague light and hearing him whimper, Ana was afraid that the child could die. She saw that his eyes were going blank and his body becoming limp; then it occurred to Ana to give him a few pats on his back, which caused the baby boy to vomit a lot. After he stopped vomiting, his mother gave him some chamomile tea, so he could fall asleep. Later in life, it was important to note that one eye would not focus properly whenever he fell ill. Since it was Huicho, no one bothered to have the eye problem checked or treated. The morenito grew up, and years later, although he was not creative but quite academically qualified and motivated, he graduated from a university. After graduation, to honor his parents, he introduced his partner to them because he decided that women were not for him. That was a great surprise to his parents. His mother who always wanted a girl and his father who was very proud of the manliness of the sons that God had given him as a reward for being himself, Don Ira, were crushed and dumbfounded.

Rafi, the youngest of the family, was the *pylon*, the "extra," and for a change, he was the spoiled child. He became the favorite of his parents by being born blonde or light-haired. Though they hoped for more children, Rafi was the last. He closed out the production of children. The cherub was born in the city, and the only one born in a hospital bed. The doña wanted to continue having more children, or as she said, "To continue to the end." The doctor had suggested that she stop having children. She was already tired and completely worn out physically. By the time of Rafi's birth, Doña Igna had lost all her teeth from a severe calcium deficiency and suffered pains in her bones and joints from the same deficiency. Unhappily for Doña Igna, she had to cut her long hair, of which she was justly proud of, to retain as much calcium in her body as possible. As a favor, the doctor had tried to make it a tie down when the cherub was born, but she awakened during the attempt and ran away from the operating table. Months later and with the push of the family, the lady finally decided to stop the baby production and had her tubes tied.

The Cherubim, as some called Rafi, became the dearest treasure of Lady Igna. She devoted herself to taking care of him and took numerous pictures to decorate the house, creating a gallery. She treated him as if he were the only son she had given birth to. The cherub was the only one who drank fresh milk. He was a spoiled brat. Igna bought him his first bike and a pet. He was the only one who did not sleep on the dirt floor like Ana had for twelve years since, for being a girl, she did not *deserve* a decent bed. From being so spoiled, the boy did not develop much of an intellect. According to his mother, that did not matter. Doña Igna said that by being so cute, he would find a woman who would not mind working to financially support him. Such a woman would not mind because she would have picked up a keeper, a truly wonderful man. His mother's comments proved true when the cherub found a woman with honor, the honor to support him. She joined Rafi to form the cherub's family.

Don Ira wanted a big family and also had his own story, a story that explains some of his actions and life views but does not excuse them. He was, he said, the youngest of eight children, but his children met none of their uncles since the siblings had died at the hands of gunmen who sought revenge on Don Ira's family. The assassinations were over some forgotten quarrel involving both families' somewhat distant ancestors. Only the revenge for the long-forgotten slight remained in memories. Ira, as the youngest, was either ignored or forgotten in the killing spree. Don Ira also had three sisters who had married young and had left him alone to care for his ailing mother until her death. Living as he did forced him to search for a woman who would take care of him. Don Ira did not feel that he was ready to marry at age twenty-five, but his needs impelled him to procure a companion.

THE BEGINNING OF
THE ORDEAL

Ira wanted a family and surveyed the local eligible young ladies and finally selected the one. Bingo! He found Doña Igna, the youngest daughter of Don Greg. He started courting her, unbeknownst to her father, because Don Greg jealously guarded the reputation of his daughters. Don Greg, Igna's father, was a man greatly respected and wanted his daughters to find a good husband who was hardworking, honest, and intelligent, and hopefully, wealthy. A man not easily found on that poor ranch. Poor Don Ira did not think along the same lines as Don Greg. He only needed a woman who would take care of him, and he had high expectations, setting his eyes on the younger daughter of Don Greg. Don Ira just had his needs. Somehow, he had convinced Ms. Igna that although he did not have money, he loved her, and his intentions were both good and honorable. He promised that while living with him, she would not lack for anything. Don Ira, after writing some affectionate letters, finally convinced the young lady that he was the man that she needed to supplement her life.

Doña Igna, on the other hand, had no experience with the outside world, since Don Greg heavily sheltered his daughters and allowed his daughters to leave his house only in the care of a proper chaperone, *if* he would allow them to attend parties away from his house. Don Greg provided his daughters with the basics, and he hoped that they would marry a husband who, like their father, would provide his daughters with the basic necessities. With Don Greg, his daughters lacked for nothing. Don Greg's customs and traditions were very conservative because he descended from an aristocratic

Spanish family who had lost everything during the years of the 1910 Revolution. As a result, Don Greg had to survive by his intelligence and hard work, but Doña Igna, being the youngest of the daughters, had no appreciation for her father's work in overcoming the hurdles that provided a good home and the necessities to shelter her from the struggles and poverty many others faced. What she resented most, according to her, was not having the love of her mother, who died when she was still a baby. Throughout her life at home, her sole interest lay in fulfilling the maternal void with affection. When Don Ira began courting her, she thought that marrying him would fill that emptiness in her heart that had lain there much of her young life.

While Don Greg was very cautious of potential suiters and was, as mentioned, a good provider for his daughters, the daughters were not very happy with the comforts and security provided by their father. Behind his back and looking for what his daughters believed to be a better life, they began to escape one by one when they came of age. Don Greg's villa was surrounded by a high fence, which safeguarded his property and kept his daughters from leaving what they saw as a prison without his permission. However, the height of the fence did not matter once a girl was bitten by the love bug. The girls would scale the wall, fleeing with whomever they saw as their savior or owner. Too late, each girl would learn that the new life with her new husband outside the wall was to give birth to children for him and serve her husband as he saw fit.

Whenever one of the girls escaped, Don Greg became a stricter disciplinarian and made rules, shackling the remaining girls to their father's will. This lifestyle was definitely not for Doña Igna. She quickly became bored with her life at home and angry at the restrictive rules imposed on her. Her activities were limited to swinging on her garden swing and doing a few chores in the compound. What occupied her consciousness daily was the hope that one day a prince charming would rescue her from her confinement. Her prince would take her for long walks and to magnificent dances where they would dance the night away. Her older sisters who had also suffered from the loss of their mother, though they cared for each other and schooled Doña Igna in the skills and duties a housewife, made a big mistake. It was a sin of omission in Doña Igna's lessons on woman-hood. According to Igna, when they jumped the fence and fled with their lover, they stopped Igna from having a remote possibility of finding a good suitor at the foot of the wall. When she met Don Ira and he offered the sky, the moon, and the stars, she did not hesitate to accept the world he offered and, like a dove looking at an open cage door, fled from the world where she had a roof over her head and good food on the table into the unknown world of his prom-ises and her dreams. Not really knowing better and not having any guidance, she had decided to take the chance and jumped into the uncharted waters with both feet.

With his perceived gallantry and several affectionate letters, Don Ira was able to persuade Doña Igna to embark on a new adven-ture, filled with nothing but promises and a young girl's fantasies. A part of the false world he created for the young, naïve Igna, were promises to take her to parties, to see new places, and to go to an occasional dance. Continuing to feed her fantasies, he invited her to begin a new life in which she would be queen of the house and, most importantly, a life in which she would no longer have to take orders from Don Greg. Not knowing that she had traded one dictator for another, because Ira never told her that he would be the one would be giving orders thereafter, she agreed to go away with Don Ira, her "prince charming"! Filled with good intentions, the couple planned their getaway. With the help of several friends and a moonless night, Don Ira, the prince of her dreams, rescued the princess from her cloister. She escaped by jumping over the fence to a new life.

The morning after the getaway, Doña Igna awoke to a harsh reality, though not yet the full reality. After a month of living together, she learned what destiny had reserved for her. Instead of gaining freedom, she gave birth to many children. Instead of a home where the cheese wattles hung from a beam in the barn, where giant pots of honey were always full, where the canned fruit was always on the shelf, and the grain and the milk from both goats and cows always awaited her, she found only a poor hovel and nearly empty shelves. The more Igna compared what she had left and had taken for granted in her life with her father, the more overwhelming her new life appeared. To make matters worse, she lost her menses, another lesson unlearned and not taught her by her sisters. It was that unspoken lesson of what happens when a woman first joins her body to a man. To make up for unspoken lessons, Don Ira had planned for a wedding, though a poor one, but a wedding nonetheless.

Another lovely surprise awaited. Don Ira, after the wedding, ordered his new wife to put away all her makeup, her tight clothing, and her high heels. At the same time, he told her to keep her jewels out of his sight; Don Ira's reasoning was seeing her with those ornaments and clothes in their new home made him very unhappy because he could not provide such items. To complete the wedding ceremony, as was the local custom, they had to apologize to the father of the bride. Doña Igna thought that at least the apology would give her a safe haven if her new life did not go well. On the chosen day, soon after the wedding and the establishment of their home, they called forth their courage in preparation of visiting Don Greg to beg his forgiveness. Envision the usual scenario, the couple would see the father of the bride seated at the back of the room, and the couple would approach him, falling to their knees before him. If Don Greg accepted their act of contrition and everything worked as they hoped, they would be dismissed, not returning until he called them to his presence. However, if Don Greg rejected their act of contrition and sent them away unforgiven, they must return to try again until everything was resolved to *his* satisfaction. As good luck would have it, Don Greg forgave them; however, he warned them that he had better not hear any crying or complaints about their decision. That was his blessing, not a warm, inviting admonition to seek his advice.

A few months later, Doña Igna noticed that she had gained a lot weight and that her small waist had disappeared. Worried, she sought reasons for these changes and sought answers from the village healer. When she consulted the *curandera*, the "healer," she learned that she was pregnant, and she would soon give birth to a baby. The healer, noting the look of surprise on another expectant mother's face, explained very patiently what happens when a couple lives together. The shock of that lesson, another untaught lesson by Igna's sisters, was almost greater than learning she was pregnant. She was very concerned about how and when the pregnancy would come to an end. The new mother just could not understand how the creature would come to the world. Doña Igna justified her ignorance by saying that she was a daughter of family; in those days, the daughters of family were not supposed to know too much about those wifely duties nor were they to ask any questions about the intimacy of couples. Those young ladies, when they married, were completely blind to the realities of a couple's intimacy and the process of procreation. As custom dictated, the more innocent the young ladies were, the more desirable the maidens became as potential brides. The reason, so people said, was that the husband would better appreciate them and even more men would respect them.

DISAPPOINTMENT BECOMES A LIFESTYLE

The following years shredded Doña Igna's dream of freedom and happiness, big words that would never again be mentioned in the bosom of the family even by chance. As the years went by, eventually, Igna lost all hope of a more comfortable and normal life. Her days were spent listening to songs that only fed the grief growing in her heart; her smile gradually faded until it finally disappeared altogether, joining the ideas of going to a dance or having fun in the graveyard of broken dreams. Her slender body grew disfigured, lumpy due to the forced labor of all those births. She was so worn that she could no longer imagine she had swung on that swing in her father's garden. She could no longer remember the boredom of her youth. In her new home, it yet saddened her daily to put her beautiful long hair up in a bun, so no one would appreciate it per Ira's request. When she ended her child production, her once beautiful white teeth were almost completely gone, and her skin, once so smooth and healthy, was now dry and stained from a lack of healthy food and restorative rest.

At some point, she was never sure of the exact moment Igna realized that her father was right when he warned his children that marrying a poor peasant without education, vocation, trade, or purpose would only earn her a life filled with torture and deep suffering. When those thoughts overwhelmed her, she also, deep down in her soul, would believe the promises of Don Ira even while reality was slapping her in her face. Doña Igna refused to believe her reality but accepted it. Almost every day, she remembered the comfortable life at her father's home that had enough food on the shelf; warm shelter on cold, stormy nights; and a full wardrobe of dresses. In contrast, in her husband's house, she would barely survive day by day by doing magic with the few items on the shelf and through the willpower of survival. Igna had to stretch everything to manage what little income Don Ira brought home. Her only hope, weakly entertained, was that her beloved sons would grow up and eventually compensate her for all her life's efforts and sacrifices. Don Ira, on the other hand, had quickly forgotten the promises he had made to Doña Igna and concentrated solely on his needs and responsibilities. To meet his perceived needs and responsibilities, Don Ira worked from sunrise to sunset in sowing season. When there was little work in the field, he would order Igna to prepare his best clothing prior to going out to distract himself from just sitting at home on *dominguear* or weekends. He would leave while the poor lady stayed home to meet her obligations as a homemaker. That treatment represented a total insult to Igna, who felt like a total fool for believing that that man would ever take her out. On weekdays, Don Ira arrived home tired and in a bad mood from the milpa, even hitting the children who simply dared to approach him.

The couple was only slightly content when the children were babies and glad that the infants did not annoy them. Doña Igna loved her children only briefly, in the moments when she thought that someday they would provide her with a life of ease and comfort as compensation for all she had given the family. With those attitudes, it was no wonder that the couple was almost always tired and cranky because they viewed life as cruel and so unfair.

As part of their thinking of life as cruel and unfair, Igna had to become the woman who covered her husband's basic needs. Don Ira's thoughts took a distinctly different track. He thought because God had removed his brothers from earth, it was Doña Igna's responsibility to *recover* them by giving him all the boys she could deliver. Throughout the marriage, compromise and responsibility for family was expected from Lady Igna. She must first, serve and please her husband and, secondly, give him many children to fill the emptiness his deceased brothers had left. Neither had the idea that the children they were bringing into their world had their own needs, nor could they fathom the idea that it would not be easy to satisfy those needs, especially if their children lived in a world of crippling poverty. Throughout the early years of marriage, Don Ira presented his wife to the other peasants, telling them that he deserved a young and fertile woman who would give him good healthy children. Meanwhile, throughout their marriage, Doña Igna was swallowing her frustrations and burning desires to describe for the other peasants the truth of what appeared to be a "happy family." In reality, it was only the appearance of one.

Don Ira expected his children to grow big and strong, to be hard workers. Don Ira needed to recover his investment through his efforts of giving them deprivation, of giving them a poor roof, and of giving them poor meals. He often said, "No matter that today I work much, when they grow up, they are going to pay with large bale of money." It never did occur to him that in his dreams of being an alchemist, that is, of magically transforming his sons into sources of wealth and property, those little ones he hoped to transform would need good nutrition and education to earn enough to repay, at least somewhat, his investment. Don Ira, like many poor and uneducated people believed that success was a magic wand and that formal education was for lazy people or people who could not or would not work with their hands. He was sure that parents only had to educate their children by example. For Don Ira, education was complete if children learned the five vowels, learned numbers from one to ten, and could sign their name legibly. He hinted that all other education would come by osmosis, but not in those words.

Don Ira's philosophy on food and nutrition was very simple. Children did not live to eat because the children were not "pigs fattening to prepare for butchering and the table." Children had to eat very little to be light on their feet, to work quickly. Don Ira did not follow his own adage. He was the first to sit at the table and did not stop eating until he was full, his appetite satiated. He justified his eating by saying that he had to eat well because he was the one who worked hard to support the family by bringing sustenance for the house. While he was served a bowl of stew with meat and sometimes having seconds, the children would often have only broth with bits of tortilla. While he drank a cup of boiled milk, the children drank a cup of tea with a small dollop of milk. As a result of his self-serving philosophy on nourishment, his malnourished children always took longer to work and did not move fast to fulfill their chores, but the order/rule was always the same, "Those who do not work, do not eat." The children continued to work, and Don Ira continued to fail to understand why they took so long and moved so slowly in carrying out their appointed tasks.

IN SEARCH OF A BETTER LIFE

The long awaited day had arrived when the family began the search for a better lifestyle. To Ana, that day seemed as if it would never come amid life's troubles. The day dawned when Don Ira realized that it was time to get out of the quagmire of that ranch, which offered only sadness and tears. It too was a time when some relatives came from the big city to try to convince Ira that migrating to the city would give the children a somewhat better life. After thinking over and over again of the benefits of leaving versus the lack of advantages of staying, he decided to at least to see for himself. First, he went solo to the city and found a job in a factory. After a month of work, he saved enough money to come back to the ranch and pick up his starving family. On that day, the family packed up their *tiliches*, their belongings, and made final preparations for the new journey. The next day, everyone awakened very early with tight stomachs gripped by both nervousness and the vague hope of a better life in an unknown world far away from the only home they had ever known. Once everyone boarded the bus, no one wanted to look to what was left behind. Perhaps, the family thought that by looking back, their departure would be more painful. The bus slowly pulled away, taking the family on a journey that would last for at least twelve hours but last for the rest of their lives.

Arriving in the city with its loud noise from the constant traffic and its many people, the poor family was simply stunned. They were so exhausted that no one even asked for or expressed anything. Standing on the sidewalk, looking about, and starving from not having eaten anything in twelve hours, it appeared to the family that they had been freed from a concentration camp to an open world outside the gates with no direction to their life. Ana was not expecting the home to which the family moved in. It was a much smaller space than what they had at the ranch and resulted in much more crowding than what she was used to. A nephew of Don Ira did him the favor of renting him two rooms. One room would be used as the bedroom, and the other would be the kitchen and dining room. As they moved their belongings into their new home, Ana thought, "Well, probably only a temporary move because things would improve soon." That hope proved to be wishful thinking.

As what always happens where there were many people and many children in a new environment, problems began to pop up, as the kids worked to adapt to their new world. One of the first problems that came to light was getting used to the new and limited space that had no patio in which to play or a place to run. It quickly became a very chaotic situation. The children fought with the other children living in the other half of the house, and the adults grew more and more frustrated, not knowing how to resolve the conflict fairly and rationally. To make matters worse, only three months after arrived to the city, Don Ira and Doña Igna decided to continue their familiar and usual pattern of having more children. Quickly, Doña Igna was pregnant again! There was no awareness on the parents part of some of the hardships that the children faced, especially having the children all slept on a cement floor. The parents seemed utterly clueless. The parents, in addition, seemed unaware that Don Ira's wages, the wages of an unskilled worker, would barely provide the most basic needs of his current family. Coupling the hardships and the cost of living with the parents bringing another human being into a world in which the family did not know if there would be enough food for another day—not to mention a drink of a glass of milk or juice—without worrying or getting anxious about it was close to insanity. Unfortunately, insanity was not the reason for having children, ignorance was. For the family from the ranch, the crisis continued and would soon intensify.

After long, ongoing conversations that never came to major conclusions or decisions, Don Ira and Igna decided it was time to move their big family that had another member on the way to a home that was hopefully larger. After a short search, the family found another home, but one similar to the one in which they were living. The drawback was that the family now shared the living space with a strange family that used the common wall as a division of both residences. Again, the second home was only two rooms, one for sleeping and one for cooking and eating. The move did not improve living conditions. There was again not enough space for the kids to sleep on the cold hard floor of the main room. Some of the kids had to sleep in the kitchen corner. However, no one complained about the accommodations since the family was thankful they were not homeless like so many others who had abandoned the rural life. No matter the living conditions, the parents continued having more babies as if there was nothing else in life to do.

FROM THE SMALL JUNGLE
TO THE BIG JUNGLE

When it became time to send the children to school, complaints echoed through the rafters, mostly from Don Ira, who had to buy the required school supplies and the mandatory uniforms for the kids. Where in the world would he get the money for such things as rare as money was in the city was a lament often heard in the house, but life had to continue as if there were no problems. Reluctantly, and with much sacrifice, Don Ira bought the uniforms for the kids, but he sternly warned them that they had better not ask him for anything more. Since nothing more meant there would be no money for lunch or snacks at school, the kids had to drink a cup of tea and eat a few animal cookies at breakfast and eat nothing more until they got home, hoping there might be something more nutritious for the evening meal.

The first day of class was a real adventure. First, Ana and her siblings had to find their places among the ranks of students at the school. She and her brothers had never seen so many kids in one place at one time. The lines were endless. Ana, gazing about in a state of awe and mild disbelief, thought, "Where did so many people come from?" It was a real conundrum finding her place in the long line. Ana's teacher, with a look of disgust on her face, told Ana to take any place in the first row, since Ana, due to malnutrition, did not grow as she should have. Although Ana was one of the oldest, she was placed with the shortest children in the row. They were a year or two younger than she was.

Added to her humiliation of being placed with children much younger was having to cope with the teasing from the other students, who obviously noticed Ana's lack of socialization skills and her second-hand clothes. In addition, Ana had to learn to speak without the accent of the newly transplanted rural and learn to speak with the lingo of the city. Finally, she had to deal with a teacher who had a very bad temper, a temper similar to a thousand demanding demons and who was easily bothered by everything from the appearance of the students to their slow learning abilities and lack of skills. To compensate for all the shortcomings and for the trauma of moving to a new arena, Ana soon realized that the only way to avoid problems was to make her life and manners more acceptable and to stay quiet most of the time. In short, Ana would keep a very low profile for a while. Although Ana had a good memory and tried to learn as much as possible as quickly as possible, she could not avoid the teacher's scolding for the slightest thing.

On one occasion, the teacher asked all students to do a summary of the history of Helen Keller. The report requirements were to put the date in the upper right side of the sheet, save the corresponding margins, and sign the summary at the bottom right of the page. With tension and nervousness rising to a fever pitch under the teacher's penetrating gaze, most of the students had forgotten at least one of the report's requirements. When the papers were collected and the teacher spotted the error, he did not hesitate punishing the entire class. He formed them outside of the classroom and shamed them before all, and one by one, he hit them on the hands with a yardstick. It did not matter that the stick and the words hurt; the teacher just berated them as he beat them with it.

Some students deliberately irritated the teacher while some just bothered him. At some, he threw blackboard erasers; at others, he pulled from their seats, dragging them to the front and making them count the number of times he would pull their hair. He did not care if the troublemaker were a girl or boy. He called them all idiots. The strongest punishment came when the teacher had pulled the hair of a student and he got a louse on his hand. The teacher then ordered all students to step outside the classroom and check each with two pencils. After checking each one thoroughly he ordered everyone to cut his/her hair to the scalp. No children could resume class if they did not comply with his orders. The next day, the boys returned to class with the shaved heads and the girls with very short hair. The teacher saw them and made fun of everyone.

The punishment seemed very cruel to Ana, who tired of the abuse that she saw at school after enduring so much abuse at home, called and found a way of asking for a hearing with the principal. By good luck or by circumstance, the principal agreed to meet with her. With fear clinging to every word, her heart trying to jump out of her chest, Ana explained in great detail what was going on in that classroom. She knew she was taking a risk. If the abusive teacher discovered her action, he might expel her from class. Ana hoped that with the meeting on Friday, the teacher would forget what she had done if the principal brought the issue to his attention.

No one mentioned anything the next week about Ana's visit with the principal. Ana, however, felt guilty for talking with the principal and tried to hide the guilt she felt for doing so. Apparently, the teacher did not discover her action; or if he did, he would definitely have been warned to mistreat students no more. She had no need to worry. To everyone's surprise, when the students walked into the class that week, there was something different. Instead of their regular teacher, another teacher stood before the class, which was the reason there were no violent outbursts on the part of the regular teacher. A week passed, and the nag teacher did not return to class. Everyone wondered what could have happened. Since Christmas break was fast approaching, the vacation, according to Ana, would help sort things out or, at least, cool things down.

When the students returned to class after the Christmas and New Year's vacation, all the children noticed a calmer atmosphere and a substitute teacher. Although some asked what might have happened if the cranky teacher were to return, there was not real answer. Near the end of the school year, the grouchy teacher did return. His head was shaved, and his facial expression was also quite different. His attitude was better than earlier in the year. After overhearing whispered comments and getting some direct questions from the students, he explained, as simply as possible. A brain surgeon had taken a piece of his brain from the corpus callosum that unites the two hemispheres of the brain, and that helped him smooth out his temper. For all students, the news sounded like a glass of cool water on a hot summer day. The teacher's short visit came at the end of the school year. As Ana headed home that day, she felt very satisfied with her year and relieved from the worry of being successful. Looking again at her report card, she was delighted to have placed among the top five students based on their overall scores. She was also satisfied that her efforts had somehow managed to calm the teacher and improved the learning environment.

THE LARGE FAMILY
LIVES WORST

While satisfaction and relief accompanied Ana's school life, the crisis continued at home with the birth of the newest member of the family. Don Ira, looking at living conditions, had decided to find another place to live. Since he could not find or could he pay for a bigger or better home, he rented half of another house with two bedrooms. In one bedroom, Don Ira and Doña Igna put their bed and barely had room for the boys on the floor. The lack of space in the bedroom left Ana to sleep in a corner of the kitchen on a floor colder than an iceberg and harder than the previous floors. The sleeping accommodations were not important, propagation at its peak was important.

The birth of the newest member of the family was quite an event for Don Ira and Doña Igna. For the rest of the family, seeing the situation in which they lived, the event was not received quite as happily. Considering the numbers and financial situation at home and of Igna's overall health, the doctor, aware of those things, had advised Igna to stop calving (not his words). Not only was her body completely worn out from repeated pregnancy, but the poor lady had, by that time, also lost all of her teeth. The doctor even strongly advised her to cut her hair. Her once long, thick, silky beautiful hair had become thin and brittle and was draining calcium from her body as her having so many children had done. The doctor could not imagine how the whole family lived though he probably guessed and accurately so. If he had known for sure, he could have suffered a stroke. The lady argued with the doctor about his intruding into her private life. Listening to her intransigence, the doctor devised a plan to counteract Doña Igna's resistance.

When the lady was heavily sedated at the hospital during delivery, the doctors would take her to the operating table to tie her tubes. This would stop her from bringing more children into the world of poverty and deprivation in which her other children lived. However, the doctors did not know of the lady's cunning. After giving birth to so many children, she did not fall asleep after the childbirth. The nurses, thinking she was asleep, wheeled her to the operating room. Igna, not completely asleep, jumped off the table and, without thinking of the risk, rushed out of the operating room, insulting everyone.

Given the circumstances of her behavior, the hospital discharged Lady Igna from the maternity ward, allowing her to return home with her new offspring. To make the situation worse, the people who came to visit her kept saying that that she should not stop calving because the cherub was so beautiful. None of the visitors were thinking about the rest of the family's wellbeing. Since she was convalescent, Igna could not even attend Ana's elementary school graduation. Her reasoning dictated that she not carry the baby to such an event. Another reason hinted in Igna's refusal. Probably the real reason behind her not attending was that Igna was focused almost full time on caring for the little one whom she had given birth to. Her focus was hard to understand because just thinking about the baby's eating every few hours would give her a headache. For comfort, she would play with the cherubim and would constantly take pictures, like portraits of him. She placed the finished photos in the home to form a gallery. In the single room where all the other children slept, that gallery told the children that the only child who mattered was the cherub.

Don Ira, since arriving in the big city, hated having to pay rent and thought of building his own home. Keeping the idea of his own home in the forefront of his mind with the topic of birth control intruding now and then, he eliminated one topic that was bothering him by agreeing to have Doña Igna's tubes tied to stop calving. Accepting the surgery as if it were a great sacrifice, Lady Igna had an episode of severe depression, possibly because she was giving up the one thing she did very well. During her depressed state, she did not want to know anything about anyone else in the family. Ana and other family members were responsible for caring for each other while Igna recovered. During that period, as usual, there was little to eat. To provide food and other necessities, Ana sought what work a twelve-year-old might secure. She was thinking she might be employed to help with household chores in the big houses. Ana did not think about the shame associated with cleaning or helping with household chores; she only cared about eating better than what she was eating at home. After school, caring for her siblings and helping with chores, Ana still had enough time to visit the rich houses to see if she could run some errands or be of personal assistance or, at least, to do dishes to earn a little money.

During the time Ana was searching for work, the government implemented a campaign of urbanization. A major part of their program was to sell federal lands that were in the foothills of the sierras. Only the poorest could buy those lands since it would take the government a long time to install the infrastructure: water, drainage, sewage and electrical services of a modern city. Don Ira, with luck finally visiting his corner, grabbed a small piece of land in the newly open area. He immediately and, in his words, with great sacrifice, built two rooms (why not three) out of cement block with a roof of galvanized sheet metal. Finally, the big family had their humble home. They did not know what kind of people would live in the new colony apart from the people being in extreme poverty. There were families with as many as twenty children, all malnourished and uneducated, living in *ticuruches*, "shacks made of cardboard sheets." Next door to Don Ira's family lived an old lady with two adult children who were both ugly and smelly. Next to them lived a prostitute who fought all the time with her clients and had several deformed children. When Ana thought about that rotten world full of such people, she could not avoid wondering why Don Ira laid claim to such a depressing place to build his home. Don Ira's only answer was that the place was the best he could afford in order to provide for his family. If the home was not good enough for Ana or if Ana was not satisfied with the living conditions, then she and the rest of children could start working to buy something better.

Don Ira, thinking his last words on the subject of living conditions was a good—no, great—idea, started sending the children, who were poorly dressed and malnourished to shine shoes and sell lemons at the market. One of the kids, possessing a beautiful, melodic voice, would use his talent, singing songs to earn a little money. Usually people gave him a few pennies for candy. One lucky day, the director of the local kindergarten heard him singing and felt sorry for the poor waif. She gave him a scholarship for kindergarten registration and tuition for one year. Consequently, he was the only boy in the family to attend kindergarten and to continue school with very good grades. Throughout elementary school, he got excellent grades and won the privilege to travel to important points in the Mexican Republic. Only after earning that honor were the parents of the little brown morenito proud of him.

FROM GUATE-MALA TO
GUATE-WORSE

Living without drinking water, without a bathroom, without toilet tissue or other basics filled the picture Ana had of a future living where she was. She summed up her thoughts by describing her past and future without change as just trying to survive on a subsistence level while not committing any kind of criminal atrocity. Ana, however, did see a different road, a road on which the best thing to do was for her to continue going to school, learning as much as possible for as long as she could. With a solid plan in place, Ana could now live with the blows, the scolding and insults, realizing they were only temporary because school and its lifeblood—education—would be the escape route. While enduring, she managed, against the winds and tides of life, to continue attending school and, at the same time, helping with the chores at home. In the morning, she helped with the house cleaning, dishwashing, and babysitting, as well as the bringing of water from the pipe when the water did not reach her street that day. Sometimes, she did not have time to eat before leaving for school and would not eat at school either. Due to hunger and fatigue, she was almost asleep during class while she was doing her assignments. However, even being so sleepy, she was able to correctly answer the teachers' questions. In the evening, after chores, Ana had to do homework by whatever light was available because there was not enough time during the day. With all the obstacles and roadblocks, Ana was able to score not only at the top of her class but also at home.

Ana enrolled herself in high school after elementary school because her parents did not see any reasons for continuing education beyond elementary school. With her excellent grades, no one questioned her application for enrolment and was accepted her into school for the next term. Along her path to success, Ana knew that the only way to find a good, well-paying job in the future would be through education. She continued to work hard to maintain top grades. Her efforts bore fruit when she graduated from the first year of high school, placing second in class of forty-five students. The first chair student, Dalia, came from a family who owned a grocery store. Ana, thinking at the time, that given Dalia's background, a good diet helped Dalia a little with her studies. In retrospect, Ana thought to herself, "Sometimes students who are hungry just do not, perhaps cannot, comprehend the lectures, and their ideas pass by like the wind. Too this day, Ana wonders how her life would be if, at least, she could have eaten meat, drunk milk, and snacked on fruit and fresh vegetables every other day as she was moving toward adulthood.

When Ana entered the second year of high school, she faced another challenge, a very aggressive teacher who was in charge of her group. The teacher always wore tight denim pants on a pretty stocky body. If someone saw her from behind, that person might think she was a strong man. To complete the picture, she wore her hair very short and used no makeup. Her presence, rather than inspiring respect, instead intimidated students. She told her class that she was an attorney but became bored with the practice of law and thought a better and more exciting career for her was teaching history and civics. In school, the common practice was to administer the routine exams every other month. That teacher tested her students each month. When she gave the first exam to the group, she failed nearly everyone. Students in the class with the highest grades in their first year of high school were the only ones who passed with a score of 8 out of 10. That result did not meet Ana's expectations.

When Ana saw her score, she was very disappointed and became sick to her stomach. She just could not understand how someone who did not know her well could possibly insult her by giving an 8 when she had always earned a 10. Deciding to find out, Ana confronted the teacher. The other students remained quiet when they saw Ana, with disgust written all over her face, march to the teacher's desk. When Ana asked her teacher for a logical explanation for her score, the teacher became very angry, and said, "So you think you're a very smartass?" and then asked Ana to recite the twenty-nine individual guarantees of the Mexican Constitution. If Ana could do so, then the teacher would see if Ana deserved a higher rate. Ana asked how much time she had to memorize them, and the teacher gave her a week. The following week, the students waited with much anticipation and some fear for the teacher's challenge. When the moment of truth arrived, the teacher asked Ana to stand before the class and recite the twenty-nine individual guarantees of the Constitution. Ana, on trembling legs, recited the guarantees successfully. Everyone hoped that Ana would collapse under the pressure, but Ana did not hesitate for a second. Once started, Ana recited all twenty-nine without interruption. The students were astonished and speechless. The teacher seemed impressed.

Even with Ana's recitation, the teacher was still put off by Ana's affront and asked Ana, by next week, to learn all the names of the most important countries on the world map and name their respective capitals. The teacher suspected that Ana would not accept the challenge without question. This time, the teacher charged all the students learn, at least, the countries of each continent. So that the assignment would not be overwhelming for the class, she separated the class into study groups, assigning a continent to each small group of students. No one escaped her latest mandate. Everyone hated Ana since her boldness forced the entire group to really put time into their studies. Since mental exercise apparently hurts, they had to blame someone for their pain. The following week, the teacher did not ask Ana to do her recitation but, instead, did a more comprehensive review and gave the students a shorter test. When assessing the exam's results, the teacher was surprised again. Ana had scored 95 percent in the exam while some students barely earned a passing score and a few never reached 50 percent. At that point, the teacher decided not to challenge Ana again and, when the year was over, told her, "You have a good future. Do not give up."

When Anna graduated from high school, her mother would not attend since she had no time for nonsensical events. Ana's father, on the other hand, sympathized with his daughter and sat among the parents who were interested in their children's graduation from high school. The school had assigned as master (actually a mistress) of ceremony the teacher who had given Ana headaches. When it was Ana's turn to receive her diploma, the teacher shook her hand and said, "Congratulations! You will achieve something someday." Later the teacher greeted Ana's father and said, "I congratulate you. You have a daughter with lots of character, and she is going to be someone in the future."

To which Ana's father replied, "Well, of course yes! The sons of Don Ira are none damn (not dumb)!"

The teacher smiled in acceptance and told Ana, "Now, I know where the character is coming from," and wished her good luck.

Finally, Ana, having completed high school and, entering the adult world of work, knew that with only a high school education, she would only find a job as a maid or a factory worker. Ana, realizing her current skill parameters, did successfully find a job in a factory even though in her mind, she only planned to work until she saved enough money to enter college. After working two or three months at her entry-level job, she was able to buy her first new pants and her first bed. She was just tired of sleeping on the floor. The job did not last long. After being laid off, Ana looked for work in shops and small businesses without finding anything that would satisfy her or, at least, would let her save some money for the future. Through those early days in the workforce, Ana, due to the extreme poverty in which she lived, did not dare to dream the dreams of other teens. While the girls were crazy about boys and dreamed of growing older and to seeing themselves as part of the perfect couple, Ana just wanted to grow and to learn as much as possible. She just dreamed of being able to find the solution to the poverty and ignorance that surrounded her constantly and slowly smothered her every day.

EDUCATING THE FAMILY

Despite her struggle for survival and her parents' complaints about everything, Ana strove to find some peace in the chaotic situation. From her youth, she believed it was her responsibility to help her family by telling them what life was all about. At the age of twelve, Ana first noted that the family lived day to day in a routine and immersed in a lifestyle that shielded the family from seeing a different, better way of life. At that time, there were eight children at home and one on the way. Ana tried to make some sense to the current scenario by asking her mother why the family has to live as they did. That query was coupled with a related inquiry, "Why are we not thinking of a better life?" Each time Ana asked her questions, her mother always offered the same response, "You know nothing about life…I do not know why you complain so much." Ana did not think she was complaining but was only trying to make sense of their thinking. Surrounded as the family was in their urban neighborhood by indigents, delinquents, and prostitutes, it was very difficult, if not impossible, to see the possibility of change, let alone actually making a change to prevent her brothers from becoming a part of that putrid community.

Although most of the family members had activities or tasks to complete during the weekend, Ana decided to interrupt them to give them the speech of the week, either on Saturday or Sunday morning, even though the house seemed like a mad house. On the weekend, the boys woke up late and usually turned on music or the TV to watch the soccer matches. If they did not have the music and the TV going, they had activities to finish, but most of their time was spent making noise. In addition to the noise and the chaos, Ana was tired of picking up their mess. The boys did not even pick up their dirty socks, which were left all over the living room. The boys just waited for the domestic servants. Ana, completely frustrated, and without asking the boys to turn down the radio or the TV, just did it herself. After turning off all the noise, Ana ordered them to the porch and to sit around the table. When everyone was gathered, Ana started her speech, "Life is not about working and barely making it like some nonrational animal. Life is about making yourself better than you were when you came into this world. This,"—waving her arm to show the all-inclusive neighborhood—"is not life. It is just having a messy life in a miserable place. You need to think about the future and how your life will be in five or ten years…You have to stop making excuses. You need to be the best in school, and at any activity you do, start by picking up after yourselves at home."

Most of the boys walked away, muttering about what Ana was saying. They said that the speech was nothing more than *tacos de lengua* a.k.a. talking nonsense. Ana, though hearing their comments, was not discouraged and continued trying to educate the family every week. On one occasion, her father joined the group. After listening to Ana's talk, her father said, "Poor Ana, she does not know what life is about. Just let her talk. One day, when she finds a man, he will straighten her up." Ana continued on her project of awakening her brothers and father from their poor thinking, using any trick or bit of persuasion in her weekly speech. She would force them listen to her with the power of her words and by her verbal images. Years went by, and yet Ana would continue saying, "You need to think about the future, what kind of lives you are going to live. Are you going to move on and live a better life or just live poor and ignorant for the rest of your lives?"

Ana's brothers' reply was always the same, "You are crazy, thinking life could be any different from what (meaning the life) we are living right now. You are dreaming if you think people like us can be different from the way we were born. You need to wake up! Look around you! There is nothing to what you are telling us. We live in extreme poverty because that is our destiny. We are humble and poor, and that is the way we have to live life." Ana was getting more and more stressed out because she had no examples of real people who had overcome such misery, only examples from her books.

In spite of all their resistance, Ana began teaching the boys to wash their socks and underwear by hand since the old washing machine was often broken. Ana also showed them how to make quick meals and to wash their dishes. Her mother was always against her teaching the boys basic household skills. Igna was often saying that Ana would make them gays, and it would be her fault that they would never become real men. Ana's father too was very upset about the issue. "I cannot wait to see how some man will make her stop such craziness and put her in her place."

Ana, when she heard her father's comments, answered, "Yes? When you find that person, bring him over to me, and I will teach him how to be a man."

After some progress and much derision, Ana decided to stop her speeches and just teach by example. By that time, half of her brothers had learned to pick up after themselves and make a quick meal regardless of her parents' scolding and fears. One of her younger brothers, whom Ana had not taught to be self-sufficient, learned how to cook so well that even his mother was surprised by his culinary skills. However, his father was not happy because, later in life, that brother lived with another gay man. They lived happily ever after. That lifestyle event was shocking news to his father, who thought that his boy would be just like him, a macho man who fathered many sons. Perhaps, to Ana's credit, the rest of those who followed Ana's directives eventually married good wives and had steady, happy families. Those who did not listen to Ana's advice and thought that they had done no wrong would continue to live in poverty and despair unlike their brothers, who created a better, more satisfying lifestyle.

THE IDEAL FIGURE

When Ana turned fifteen years old, she, like any girl her age, cared deeply about how she looked and measured their waist, trying to match the ideal figure. Others her age were preparing for their *quinceañera* party, a very important milestone celebration on a young girl's road to adulthood. However, Ana's parents neither acknowledged her fifteenth birthday nor asked her what gift she would like upon reaching her fifteenth birthday as other parents were doing. Nobody in the family even mentioned Ana's upcoming birthday or appeared to have the faintest intention of having a quinceañera party. Ana's mother, instead of sympathizing with Ana's concerns or nurturing Ana's self-esteem, showed Ana a beautiful dress that her mother had saved from Igna's fifteenth year. She showed Ana the dress, and in a mean-spirited move, just to rub Ana's life in her face, sarcastically said, "I had a body by the age of fifteen." It just never occurred to her mother for a moment to think that she had lived a totally different life. It was a life with a lot of nutritious food, and she, Igna, had proper, balanced meals. On the other hand, poor Ana had to eat what was left after everyone else ate. Consequently, due to malnutrition, Ana had not yet developed the body of woman. Igna asked Ana to try on the stupid dress. When Lady Igna saw 'that damn dress hanging loosely on Ana's immature body, the body without a feminine figure, Igna just smiled a very mocking smile. Igna had deeply hurt Ana's feelings again. Young Ana soon put aside her sadness. Instead, she saw a new challenge in place of a chasm of despair. Ana would show Igna that she could easily transform her body. However, Ana knew that, deep down, changing the mind of some people, people who would see her as a woman rather than a little girl, would take much longer.

As if she had not said enough, Igna repeated comments like "all young ladies" are pretty." Doña Igna would continue her venomous attacks by talking about the gorgeous body development of her nieces. In addition, Igna further attempted to undermine Ana's pride to see how she might react when Igna pointedly talked about some handsome guys. One of Igna's favorite jabs was, "Anything that resembled a man would be good enough for my favorite daughter!" When she would hear such remarks, Ana, knowing full well her mother's intentions, answered Igna's remark with words like "If I wanted them, I could have them." Ana was definitely not ready to let her hormones rule her life just like how hormones seemed to rule everyone else her age. Ana's retorts outraged Igna, who insulted Ana further by saying that Ana was probably not female enough, meaning straight or heterosexual, hinting in many ways that Ana might be a lesbian. Igna continued the disrespect by alleging that something must be wrong with her daughter because all the other girls were crazy about boys, and her daughter was not. "Ana! You are a piece of work." For years, Ana's mother would repeat the same hurtful words and spiteful comments, often ending her sermons with a time-worn admonition from the ranch: "Women have to take care of themselves and be very nice to be able to deserve the affection of a man or a husband." Igna had no a clue that Ana was constantly besieged and wooed by men when she was out in the streets. Igna seemed clueless about many things in Ana's life.

To prove Doña Igna wrong and to prove that she would develop a woman's figure, Ana got a job at a gym. The work schedule was long and arduous, seven o'clock in the morning to ten in the evening. However, she had a three-hour break at noon. During those three hours, Ana took advantage of the aerobics and weights classes offered by her employer. In less than four months, Ana managed to develop a fit, healthy looking body. She ate healthy, nutritious food at the gym's nutrition bar. With the exhaustive exercise, the stomach fat disappeared, and she developed her bust and buttocks. Once Ana knew that she had lost weight, she asked Igna for the dress her mother bragged about. Trying the dress again, it fit but was tight at the bust since Ana had developed a near-perfect bust which her mother did not have when she was a young girl. Her mother was dismissive and said to her: "That is all artificial. It is not something natural! Men will look at you from far away. But when they look closer, they will not see your natural beauty."

Ana realized at that moment that she would never please Igna, never make her mother happy for her daughter. Instead of continually insisting on proving herself to Igna, Ana moved a few steps down the road of life and decided to continue educating herself, to continue looking for better things to do with her life. Throughout the ordeals of her teen years, Ana did not fit well with her cousins because she was not husband-hunting or desirous of the vanities many women pursued. Besides, her rebellious and revolutionary ideas caused Ana to be rejected from membership into the Clan of Beauties. However, Ana did not feel any sense of rejection. She had enough faith that, one day, she would show them, but probably not convince most of them, that there are more important things in life than the nonsense of youth.

THE CLAN OF BEAUTIES

Ana noticed that many rural families had moved to the city as well, but for most, the situation and its outcome differed from that of Ana's family, as all the rural families scrambled to adapt to life in the new urban community. For instance, her cousins had found a way to not only adapt to the new life but also to ignore the shortcomings the rest of the family experienced as they adapted to the urban lifestyle, their own way of escaping the new reality. They formed the Clan of the Beauties in which the members and their activities would stay in the family. The cousins gathered at the home of the oldest cousin to talk about their adventures, their successes, their failures, individual activities, and new knowledge. At these gatherings, they also drank and danced while a few would go off by themselves *despistadas*, to practice another type of forbidden game that later would slowly reveal its consequences.

The Clan of Beauties was formed by both female cousins and male cousins as a type of private girls and boys club. Pita was the eldest. Everyone respected her because she was not involved in any so-called bad behavior. She was very hardworking and very dedicated to the house. She was the daughter of Vito, the newspaper of the ranch. Pita also helped her younger brothers as they tried to improve themselves although not everything would go as she hoped and planned. She had sacrificed her youth by working and by saving for the future. Following her quinceañera, she was not allowed to have many boyfriends like the rest of the clan. She was in her thirties and still remained a miss, a virgin as she described herself. Consequently, she was considered a role-model daughter for every young lady to follow and presented as an example by those who knew her. Most of the parents of the other cousins were not disturbed by the children being at the clan's meeting in her house every weekend.

Pita's younger brothers and sister were May, Hetor, and Mary. May and Hetor were meant to be teachers in Pita's family plan, but their minimal native intelligence did not help them reach this career goal because there was something definitely lacking in their knuckle-heads. Although they tried several times to pass the qualifying exams, they were unable to graduate from the teacher training program and ended up working in a local factory instead of the classroom. Mary, who had never been among the brightest in her class, never did develop her intellect but did develop a figure. Her other cousins said she wanted to be a commercial secretary. She and Pita thought the only skills needed to be a *secretaria* were a tall, slender figure coupled with long, abundant hair. When Mary enrolled in the shorthand and typing classes, she realized that intelligence and motor skills needed to be joined to her other assets. As much as she tried to pass these two classes, she could not master the necessary skills. She could never type quickly or accurately enough, and although attractive, she would never graduate as a commercial secretary.

With her resounding failure in educating herself, the beautiful Mary had few choices. The only option she believed left to her was to use her beauty. She hoped to find a good man who at least would consent to marry her. Beginning her job search, showing off her long hair and slender figure as a part of her resume, she set her sights on the son of the owner of the corner grocery store. The young man was a pretentious guy who hinted that he had a lot of money. Mary, who failed to see all aspects of her decision thought that if she give the guy the taste of love he asked of her that he would succumb to her ideas. She would use her beauty to hook him in a quick marriage. Big mistake! The guy took what was offered until, suddenly, the brunette began to feel ill. As the following month went by, she noticed a delay in her menses. When Mary told her prospective husband the good news, he acted just like Pontius Pilate. He washed his hands of her and ended their relationship. Mary, after option 1 failed, again only saw one other option, look to the family for support. Mary's family noticed that there was something wrong. Her behavior and physical appearance had changed. After trying several ways to find out what was wrong, they concluded that the girl was pregnant.

Pita, feeling the shame incurred by Mary's becoming pregnant, wanted to hide her face, for Pita felt somewhat responsible. She could not figure out who was responsible for "the favor." Mary convinced the family that the guy was not responsible for damages. The family created option 3, to find a solution to the problem. In those days, abortion was not a very common practice, and doctors were unwilling to perform that type of surgery. That meant the only source available to get rid of the package was to find a witch woman who would help her get rid of the problem. Mary's mother and Pita secured a witch who would help her. A few days after visiting the witch woman, Mary magically recovered her skinny figure and wore a face of repentance that only she could wear. She recovered slowly from her wrongdoing and had learned that playing with fire was not the best option to life's problems. While recovering, she decided to find a job as a secretary although she had not completed the training program. She hoped to land a job in an office. Her luck was not very good. During her search, she could only qualify for one job, a factory worker in the local factory.

After so many trials and setbacks, Mary still retained her beauty, her slim figure, and long, well-groomed hair. Working in the factory side by side with both men and women, the men could not miss her. One man who fell in love with her was so impressed with her beauty that he decided to ask for her hand in marriage. When Mary told her family about the man's good intentions, her mother and Pita decided to be honest with the future groom. When he asked them for her hand in marriage, they told him about her mistake, her misstep. Their thinking was that the man would accept her for her beauty and forgive her youthful folly. However, though poor and poorly educated, he claimed his dignity. He felt betrayed, saying he had been duped by Mary's beauty and by her not telling him of her failure/fiasco from the beginning of their courtship. In his way of thinking, Mary appeared to be in the bait business, and as a result, she could never have a decent wedding.

Given the circumstances of the event, all the decent wedding plans were scrapped. Revealing the secret forced Mary's promises to the family and dreams of herself and her mother to crash. Although the man was disappointed, he was still in love, and he continued seeing Mary. Shortly after the debacle with her mother and Pita, he proposed to forgive her sin only if she wanted to continue the relationship under his terms. The man suggested a deal although it was far from ideal. At least, his proposal would redeem her from her fault since nobody would accept her otherwise. As Mary's self-esteem was already in the mud, she felt that she was left with no other option than to accept his proposal to live with him. There was no promise of marriage. Mary accepted the proposition and went to live with the man who extended his hand to amend her mistakes. After taking her to live in a very poor and dirty place, a gross hovel as Mary's family described it, the first thing he did was to buy her in a hot dog cart and put her at a popular bus stop. It was obvious then that he had no compassion for Mary. He fathered a couple of little kids with her. That was the result of the life of one beauty in the clan.

A second group of cousins were Malen, Marty, Rodo, Soco, and Rule. They were Aunt Guani's children. All were either elementary school teachers or in training to become teachers. Malen had been the first to graduate from the teacher training program and had encouraged her brothers to pursue the same career. She was the second in command of the clan. However, as her physiological needs grew stronger, she would suddenly slip out of the Saturday night meetings to go out and have sex. The young lady soon had her first score, and to offset it, she planned a quick wedding so nobody suspected her of having a little mistake.

Marty, the next in the line of teachers, also embarked on her own adventures, soon finding a suitor whom she felt was worthy of her. When she decided to introduce her suitor to her parents, the one whom she had chosen, her parents did not approve and rejected the young man immediately. Marty, not to be denied and already independent and possessing willpower bolstered by the evidence which was about to become very noticeable, took flight with her lover and eventually married the young man, so their infant would be born into a family at the end of nine months.

Rodo, the third teacher of the family, successfully completed the studies required of a teacher. Unlike the others, Rodo was very shy and not very attractive and, in addition to what he felt were unacceptable characteristics, he stuttered. Although he could confidently gather together with the group, he found it very difficult to find a partner outside the circle of cousins, which upset him greatly. By luck, whether good or bad, Rodo found his soul mate in another cousin who also suffered from an inferiority complex. Her feelings of inferiority resulted from an eye that would wander to the side. When the two souls, each with his/her own disability, found each other, Cupid loosened an arrow that pierced their hearts. Though the world was opposed to a relationship between first cousins, the two lonely souls did not care what others might think. Following their hearts, they joined their sorrows and their bodies and were exiled from the clan.

The youngest of the string, Soco and Rule, were not physically appealing. There were no games for them. They just enjoyed chattering with the rest of the cousins due, probably, to their age and their lack of physical appeal.

The previously mentioned female cousin with the inferiority complex was Cutie. Nature was not very generous with her gifts. Nature did not bestow a sexy figure or any social grace on her. Since childhood, people ridiculed her because she had a bad eye. Apparently, her mother had taken the poor baby outside and into the cold when the young girl had a fever, causing one eye to move its focus to the side. It never came back to the center of the socket. Living in poverty as she did and having a lazy eye, Cutie could not be admitted to the education system, which was not equipped to teach students with certain disabilities. According to the parameters of the clan, her looks, her poverty, and lack of an education were real reasons that convinced her that she deserved little and would receive little in life. Consequently, Cutie found it difficult, if not impossible, to get a boyfriend until Rodo, her first cousin, accepted her. Eventually, the two fled to make a different life outside the family circle that condemned them for their sin and sacrilege. Someone who saw them after the banishment commented that they had consummated their love and produced normal children. This was a pleasant surprise since everyone expected their children to suffer Down syndrome due to the "crossing blood" of the family.

Grace was another beauty of the clan. She believed she was the reincarnation of the actress Raquel Welch or, at least, that was what the clan believed. She was the daughter of the teacher at the ranch who had taken advantage of Aunt Mar. Since Grace's father, the teacher, had taken advantage of Aunt Mar, who became pregnant, Uncle Travis threatened the teacher with grave bodily harm if the teacher would not make the situation respectable. In a word, Uncle Travis forced the teacher to marry Aunt Mar. The child, although a very pretty creature, had a small birthmark. Grace, like her father, studied and graduated as a teacher. Being educated and also beautiful, she was ahead of the game. Following in her father's footsteps, she became a very respected school teacher, which gave her the luxury of taking up or leaving with whomever she picked and changing boyfriends as often as one changes her underpants. Base instinct is sometimes stronger than the intelligence, and suddenly, like other young women in the family, she "lost the moon," her menses. By living life in the fast lane, also called *la vida loca*, it was not surprising that she became pregnant. Like the others, in order to "cover the sun with a finger," Grace married quickly to give a home to the product of her sexual pursuit. After childbirth, Grace was still attractive; however, after a while, she fell in love with another loafer on a motorcycle. One day, she packed her bags and left with her new boy toy to live a life of adventure on the road, leaving the child with the father.

Guera the Blonde was the beauty who had strong desire to be an artist. One of her traits was changing her name as often as she changed underwear or *chones*. Sometimes, she called herself Johana, other times, Roxana while others knew her as Farrah Fawcett or Sandy of *Grease*, the character played by Olivia Newton-John. One time, she appeared as Yuri (the singer). She thought that men showered her with compliments, which she called flowers. However, not having much self-esteem, she did not know that the complements were all *leperadas* or obscenities. To her, they were just nice compliments. She worked as maid in the Colonia del Valle, a wealthy community. She said that she dressed as a *riquilla*, a bimbo, because she wore the clothes that her employer's daughters left for her use whenever the daughters bought new clothes. La Guera not only wanted to be just a maid in a wealthy house but also the owner of one. She said that dressing well would allow her to befriend a wealthy man and marry a junior from the Valle's community. To achieve her dream, most of her salary went toward transforming her Cinderella image into Sandy from *Grease* by purchasing two pair of satin pants—one pearl colored and one black pair—that fitted her body tightly. Lacking the cultural knowledge that went with being a member of the Valle's social class, she thought that such apparel was for everyday use when, actually, such attire was only used when dancing at the disco. That style of dress on the street caused the jerks on the street corners to shout leperadas at her. Since she received a few positive compliments, she just accepted those swear words, never realizing that the Sandy she saw herself becoming, in her probable delusion of at least becoming in her dreams look Nordic, a tall, slim, blue-eyed blonde who only wore such pants for the movie.

In time, Guera realized that she only gave the wrong idea to the guys in the street by dressing provocatively. At that point, she decided to reveal her beauty and her attire in the disco. Unfortunately, her dancing was compared to moving like a parrot on a hot griddle. In those times of the mania, still thinking of herself as Sandy, she met her John, calling him her friend of dance. John had another friend with a delusional, believing themselves to be to be Starsky and Hutch. That trio lived a very complicated life. She believed she had met John of *Grease*, who already had a partner, and the three saw themselves not as dancers but as actors. Nonetheless, the blonde felt like a million bucks with her two friends. Feeling confident in the partners' company, she decided to invite them to her humble home. Her father opened the door and registered shock and surprise, which really surprised her. When la Guera presented her friends to her father, his face filled with shame.

"Hey, little girl, these men can be no friends of women." Guera's father, surveying the trio, could not make any sense of the group.

To her father's comment, she replied, "Don't be so outdated. This is the fashion now."

Her father asked, "When will my crazy girl get sane?" As her behavior continued, her father continued to ask himself the same question until one day he added, "It appears like she will never get herself together."

Continuing with her belief in her being beautiful because she was Guera, she thought being a typist was a very sexy career. She also thought it would not be difficult to land a good job as a secretary. Off to school she went, earning a certificate in typing. So began her secretaria career. Before beginning her new career, she believed she was a "something out of this world" After being promoted in her new endeavor, she saw herself as no longer the divine crane but had become "the royal eagle." She would buy branded perfumes and arrange her hair with highlights, and use fine makeup. She thought she would win an executive and humiliated any man that dared approach her, that is, any man who did not have high status to offer. What the chiefs offered, however, were only indecent proposals. The suitor she was looking for was not among the executive class. Though it took guera some time, she finally convinced herself that prince charming was not on the horizon, either distant or near. So it was back to school to continue her preparatory studies in a night school for workers. She wanted to study to become an attorney. After, completing her studies and graduating from preparatory school, she enrolled into the school of law. Still, the blonde was having a hard time finding her prince charming. Instead, she found her little giant.

The blonde (guera) thought that she was the only one in the night school who would attract attention from the men in her classes, but she soon realized that there were others like her who were looking to attract attention. She wore her secretary's uniform to class in hopes of impressing her teachers and dreamed of enticing one to marry her. As part of her hunt, she would take pictures with them to see if they expressed any interest in her. In her imagination, she fantasized that those who did her the favor of taking a picture with her were in love with her. Later, she would discover that they only wanted to have a little fun. When she finally awoke to the reality of her photo sessions and realized the dimension of her delusion, she saw clearly the true intentions of the teachers. To compensate for the collapse of her dream and as she was very sociable, she changed directions and focused on a young man who was not on the same social or financial level as her teachers. He was one of her suitors and quite different from the rest. He, her gallant Pepin, would later become the outright owner of a successful business. At that point in his life, the poor guy had no steady job. He was one of the oldest children in a family of twenty brothers. He and his nineteen brothers had several fathers (he said his mother liked variety). When the guera heard that his family situation, that the family was both large and dysfunctional, she sympathized with him, and according to her, she would do him a favor by improving the species. Eventually, the Little Giant, as she called him because he was her height, conquered her. Later, the little giant would lead her to the altar and then to their first home, a dump as they called it. They lived there for a while until they got a decent place. They later moved to their humble home. The little giant made her a *panzoncita*, a chubby little girl. She looked exactly like him, not only physically but also intellectually. The guera had fulfilled her promise; she had improved the species.

The most exclusive cousins were the mayor's daughters, who were known as the princesses. The oldest princess, Feona, was very shy and barely talked. She appeared distracted most of the time. She would forget when asked about common things, and she would sometimes forget where she was in the world. On one memorable occasion, she forgot she was waiting at the bus stop and started sucking her finger. Nearby, people started laughing at the teenager. When she awoke to the moment, she became very embarrassed. The younger princess, Diana, was very aloof. She was not from the same social class as her family or neighbors. She did not want to mingle with the rest of her lower class cousins. The girls were two princesses who looked down on their families, each knowing she will rise above the misery of her current state in life and never suffer like the rest of the poor cousins. If only they could see the future. They would see a world crushed and broken into irreparable pieces when their father, the honorable mayor of the town, decided to abandon his perfect family to enjoy life with his secretary, who was twenty-five years his junior. The whole family was devastated! No one could understand how something like that could happen to them.

Since the family thought they were the untouchables and, therefore, very exclusive, they had few friends who would actually stick to the family. Thus, there were the two princesses, trying to overcome that bad moment of their family. The younger princess, thinking she was smarter than everyone else, was going to the university at that time. Her solution to the pain and sorrows of the family's disaster was to finish college as soon as possible, complete her legal studies, and become a lawyer. However, after graduating from college, she jumped at a new opportunity, the first opportunity offered, and just took off. No one knew why or how she found a man who seemed to have money. Later, people whispered that Diana was a missioner or the man's mistress. Sometime later, news reached the family through some relatives that she had settled in a foreign country and had started a family.

Meanwhile, the princess, Feona, could not endure the shame of her father's betrayal. As soon as she could, she contacted a well-to-do foreigner. Big surprise! Given her shyness, her apparent lack of social graces, and having barely finished high school, many were astonished that she could make such a big leap from her current family sanctuary. Regardless of the gossip and advice of many other family members, she took control of her future. She made arrangements to marry that man and flew to the USA. The local gossips said she did that because she either feared her parents' disapproval or she had already been knocked up. After the wedding and after having several children, she brought her husband and children to meet her family. Apparently, the reason for her shame or fear, according to the family gossips, was her husband's age. He was about twenty years older than she was and had his own baggage. In time the family mellowed after knowing the grandchildren, forgetting about the issue of age. After everyone's concerns were laid to rest, she started to brag about how perfect her family was even though her husband looked older than her father.

As the so carefully made plans of keeping the clan together were ripped to shreds by time and circumstance, Pita, still the director of the clan, abandoned all hope of resolving the infighting or of dealing with the pregnant members of the group. Pita finally said yes to an old boyfriend's proposal and put an end to her maiden status. She was still very young, in the full flower of her youth, when her poor boyfriend had first fallen in love with her. Pita, rejecting his proposals and being a very committed family's elder daughter, had to work until things improved. Her boyfriend would have to wait, but the man had needs and was not willing to wait until Pita was ready. He found another partner, only to realize that his heart still belonged to Pita.

When Pita turned thirty-eight, her old boyfriend, who was already divorced, came to her to recover his heart. Quickly, the wedding plans were made and finalized, not because she was pregnant but because they had already wasted too much time apart and might have little playing time left to them. In addition, they wanted to see the fruit of their love come to bear and grow to adulthood. On her wedding day, Pita looked in the mirror, and seeing herself in her wedding dress, whispered to her reflection and to those assisting her, "I leave you, dressed in white and with a head held high, and you shall do the same." What she implied, she said later, was that because she waited for marriage as a virgin, everyone else should do the same. Ana could not believe what the older cousin had said. Ana did not know to whom Pita might be referring to. Most of the cousins present already had eaten their cake before recess, meaning most of them had lost their virginity prior to getting married. Still wondering at the remark and the circumstance of her cousins, Ana thought to herself that people have their own way of being happy. What would her way of finding happiness be?

PERSISTENCE AS A
PATH TO PROGRESS

A year after Pita's wedding, Ana celebrated her sixteenth birthday but was not yet considered an adult. For employment purposes, she was not qualified to earn the minimum wage but was considered employable. In addition to not paying minimum wages, many jobs had an element of sexual harassment involved. Ana soon learned that whenever she was interviewed for work and the interviewer was a man, he would very often ask if she were sexually active. At the question, Ana blushed because she thought it was obvious that she had never had a boyfriend. She had other worries. During one interview, Ana asked why this question was asked in the interviews. The interviewer said that with the body she had, any girl would use it for its purpose. He was implying that at her age, all girls, or most of them, were governed by their sexual hormones. Whenever she asked for work in offices or stores/supermarkets, the same "offer" was always proffered. All the time she was searching for work that might pay above minimum wage, she would walk out on the interviews to pound the pavement again, hoping for another opportunity and wondering whether she would ever get a good job. Tiring of the propositions from potential employers who only invited her to a hotel instead of giving her the opportunity to work, Ana took jobs in clothing stores or small restaurants.

When Ana convinced herself that the marketplace insanity could not continue, she decided to enter preparatory school or college. With insufficient savings, she had to work at least part-time. Her decision drew more negative comments and little encouragement from her family. Family members, never missing a chance to get in a dig or a sarcastic remark, were saying that Ana was only going to college to avoid her destiny of one day marrying and having her dreams crushed by household chores, as if marriage was some type of a punishment. It became clear from their oft spoken aspersions that Ana was preparing to do the opposite, to flee from their short-sighted lives. Instead of living together with their poverty of spirit and financial shortcomings, she sought a college degree. She sought self-sufficiency and a life in which no one would throw anything in her face as she chased her other dreams. For the time being, her parents and siblings only saw things through their own lens: "To project their insecurities and doubts in the female role," to lend a voice to their ignorance and prejudices. There was not one day that her parents or brothers failed to remind her about her silly idea of attending school. They never failed to point out that it would be very difficult for her to get a job because she was poor and looked it. Ana, closing her eyes and her ears to the impediments at home, continued attending college/school. She never understood her family's criticism.

The more the family criticized her pursuit of education, the more Ana pushed back by more vigorously continuing her studies. No obstacle was too great. On one occasion, Ana arrived home from her night classes around midnight. She missed the last bus going to her neighborhood and had to take another bus to the bus station and transfer to another route. When she arrived home, everybody had already eaten. They had left the empty pans and dirty dishes for Ana to clean the next morning, if she had time before going to work and school. Ana was very hungry because all the stores were closed by the time she finished classes, and she had only eaten a bag of chips between classes. When Ana asked what was their plot was, leaving that mess for her, the family members surrounded her and told her what she was expecting to hear. As she failed to contribute much to the expenses, she ought to be thankful for being *tolerated* at home for doing nothing. Ana, being tired and hungry, flew into a rage and yelled at her parents and brothers. "Did you find me in a dump and, taking pity on the poor foundling, bring me home? It must be true for no other reason explained your contempt and lack of consideration." The oldest brother, Chino, told her to shut her mouth and screamed at her to end the tirade. He also sneered and told her that he did not believe that she was studying that late.

When her mom jumped into the ring, Igna yelled at Ana that she better find someone to support her because they could no longer pay for her food" Ana responded in a questioning tone, saying, was Igna perhaps hinting that she should follow her footsteps and end up poor and bitter with lots of kids hanging on her skirt. Chino, with a curse, told his mother, "Leave it alone, Mom. She will soon end up *panzona* (pregnant) and will have to swallow her words."

Hearing that, Ana became even more enraged and replied with venom in her voice, "Listen carefully to what I have to say because I'm not going to repeat it. What you wish upon me, and I will spell it out in simple words and sentences so you can understand it, you are going to suffer! You will suffer in shame and humiliation on what you love most!" While she talked, Chino continued to rain insults on his sister. Ana continued to rail against him, ignoring his familiar rants. She said, "Soon you will marry and will have one or two daughters. She or they will be the girl or girls of your dreams. One of them, or perhaps both, at seventeen, my age now, will make you a grandpa." Those words stopped his insults. They struck home, playing with his fears. He also remembered that was not the first time that Ana had guessed what would happen later.

Ana's father followed her brother, saying, "I said this before, women are pure waste."

Ana replied in disdain, "What a pity. To think so little of your own blood. You have forgotten that you came from a woman, and it was a woman who gave birth to all of your children."

His only response was his usual response, which means he had no other response, "You definitely deserve a beating!"

Ana replied rebelliously, "If you hit me, make sure that you kill me. If you let me live, I will continue to grow a bit more and will do the same to you. Remember, you are growing old while I am growing strong. Finally, when you need something from me, when you ask a favor of me, I'll remember this moment." The argument ended abruptly with those words, and nothing more was said. Don

Ira looked ashamed while the other family looked neutral or beaten, At that, the family, all but Ana, retreated to their beds and slept. Ana walked out on the patio where nobody would see her and cried from the rage and frustration she felt. When she had cried her rage out, she went to sleep.

A year later, Ana graduated from preparatory college and continued to expect little support from her family. She only invited an aunt and a cousin to her graduation mass. Her aunt, feeling that Ana's family should attend, spoke with Igna, who agreed to attend the graduation mass only if they would go together.

By the time she graduated from the preparatory school, Ana had turned eighteen, which increased the pressure from the family for her to work and to contribute money for food. Although jobs remained limited for her, due to lack of training and experience, Ana found a stable job and continued to save for tuition and materials prior to entering the University. She continued to give the family a little for her expenses, but for the family, her contributions, no matter how large, were never enough. Discussions by several family members on the subject of her contributing to the family coffers and to her remaining unmarried continued unabated. However, the comments became more vicious and the situation more uncomfortable when Ana told the family she was enrolling at the university the following year. First, Don Ira, speaking pessimistically, blustered, "You believe you do not deserve a man to support you since you need to study to make yourself worthy of his love." While her mother muttered, "A monkey in silk stays a monkey." Throughout, the brothers just laughed at her, saying that she had lost her mind. Their reasoning was that the university was only for those who could afford it. Their words fell on deaf ears. Ana had already investigated the cost of the books and the tuition called quotas per semester. She would not give up and enrolled herself at the university, tackling obstacles one at a time.

DAYS AT UNIVERSITY

Ana's application to the university was accepted, and she looked forward to her studies and to her first day of classes with a mixture of nervousness and excitement. Her family noticed Ana's growing anxiety about starting classes, especially on the Sunday before her first classes. That day, she reminded the family that she would start at the university on the following day. Her news received mixed reviews. Most comments were negative or demeaning.

Her father began the insults in his most eloquent style, "Women are like donkeys. The more they study, the ruder they become."

Ana replied, "Precisely. For such encouraging feedback, I go because I don't want to be a trained donkey."

Her brothers made crude jokes and comments that were definitely in bad taste. "Let's see if you can whistle or sing."

Her mother, clearly not on the same page as her daughter, rolled her eyes and said in exasperation, "Who knows what got into her mind this time."

No one offered a simple comment of moral support.

In answer to all these attempts at casting a damper on her new life, Ana answered one and all. "Just watch me!" in a forceful tone of voice as only Ana could utter. Her courage and strong front was a mask. In reality, Ana felt as if she were jumping from a high diving board into an Olympic-sized swimming pool without knowing to swim.

The first day of classes began with a case of nerves which bored a hole in her stomach. Her nerves and her fears increased as she moved from class to class. Each teacher explained the curriculum for the semester. She would read at least three or four books for every subject in addition to the text book. At the end of the day, she worried about the money to get all those books. Her day only got worse as she learned the cost of all the books. The fears careened out of control within Ana when she learned that some books were not available in either bookstores or libraries. The reading lists were the result of some teachers having studied in the US or Europe. To them, finding the books necessary to meet course requirements for the semester was not a difficult task.

After checking the cost of books again, in addition to their availability, Ana could not help thinking that her new adventure was about to crash and burn before it even started. She thought that her failure would prove her family correct about university education only being for the wealthy. Faced with certain failure and having to face her family, she grasped at what turned out to be a brilliant idea. She would visit every public library as well as the central library of the university. In one or more of those libraries, she should find at least half of the books from each subject's curriculum. Part two of her plan was to check the possibility of making copies of those books. Part three of her plan was to actually copy the books, checking the books out and copying the most important parts or, as a last resort, buy the books. When she finished making copies, she would return the books and either buy or check out the remaining required texts. Added to her reading, Ana made copies of her class notes and memorized them. When the semester exams arrived, Ana was prepared and passed with top scores. By the time Ana finished her university career, she had at least four or five cardboard boxes full of notes and copies of books.

Meanwhile, at home, the complaints continued nonstop. It had become a habit to cast remarks into Ana's face for every crumb of food she was eating. She also had to endure the hustle and bustle of everyday life in a house full of people and the lack of consideration from her brothers. The brothers would arrive about midnight if they were dating or stayed with friends after work. Their arrivals after eleven o'clock were announced by turning on the light and the TV. Admittedly, they did it just for spite. More interruptions in her much needed rest came at four in the morning when the lady of the house woke up to prepare breakfast for her husband and lunches for the children if they were working. The pungent, overwhelming smell of onion that she used to spice up the lunch always woke Ana, who had become a light sleeper from her years of caring for her brothers' crying at night during their infancy. On most mornings, Ana would awaken still very tired, as most nights found her just going to sleep after midnight. Instead of being able to get a nutritious breakfast, she had to listen to all the fuss her mother would make about not having enough for the family. Ana then would make some tea or coffee with a pinch of milk and get ready for the university. The trip to the university from her home by bus took her about two hours. She first rode a bus to the city center and, from there, transfer to a second bus, which would drop her on the main road at least two kilometers from school. She had to walk those last two kilometers. The routine was reversed at the end of the day. The commute worsened when it rained, and she had to walk in the rain to the building where she had classes. She would arrive at class soaked with her rotten shoes oozing water, which was very embarrassing. It must be noted that like all the other obstacles placed before her, a little rain would never keep her from continuing her education.

AN UNKNOWN DISEASE

Toward the end of Ana's first year at the university, her brother, Chino, was planning his wedding. Although he did not complain much about the conditions under which the family lived, Chino had begun to save. Instead of upsetting his parents with complaints and whining, he secretly had planned to elope or "to fly away" as he said. He believed himself to be a gallant, and as gallants could have any woman they wanted, he bragged about finding an ideal woman who knew how to cook and keep a good home. While on his search, he had left some women with a "present"; he had impregnated them. He believed that some of them would not be too happy about his deception of love. He was afraid that there would be women who would try to interfere with his wedding plans, specifically, to prevent his hit-and-run or fly-away nuptials. In his delusion, he predicted that at least one of the women would act out on the day of his wedding by appearing at the church and make a scene. With so much stress and nerves, Chino became ill a few weeks before the happy event. He thought that his sins had come to haunt him since he was highly superstitious and believed in those things. To rid himself of the evil spirits, he visited the healer who taught him how to cleanse his spirit and his life. To be on the safe side, he visited the local medical doctor who prescribed medicine for his illness. He never named the evil illness that had attacked him. After a week or two, the illness eased, and he resumed the preparations for the wedding to be held in two months' time. Ana watched that sequence of events cautiously. She sensed that the symptoms and the consequences of Chino's illness were not totally gone and that the illness could have side effects.

About two months before the wedding day, Ana's life would be visited by a crisis. Ana was in final exams for the second semester of her first year at the university. One morning as she was on her way to her classes, she was ravaged by a very painful, violent headache. Ana thought her headaches were caused by the stress of semester exams. Later that day, she realized her headache was more than a common headache as red and purple spots began to appear on her skin. She knew this was not normal. She spoke to the teacher, who excused her from class. She next spoke with the academic secretaries of the university to have them tell her other teachers that she could not attend her remaining classes and tests. After that, she returned home and went directly to bed. She remained in bed for the next three or four days. Rather than fielding questions about being in bed, Ana listened from her bed to her family in the kitchen. The comment, "She must be sick, but she deserves it for thinking that she could go to the university and also work, as if it were so easy" was heard in one form or another several times a day. Throughout her staying abed, nobody noticed that Ana had eaten nothing during that time. Nobody helped her as she was trying to walk by holding onto the walls to keep from falling. No one asked to see if she needed go to the bathroom. Neither her mother nor any other family member seemed to care about Ana, who lay listless and prostrate in her bed. Throughout all this, Ana only had one thing on her mind: her plans for a college education were finished. How could her dream continue when she was no longer able to eat and was only racked with fever and pain that consumed her strength and consciousness? She felt pain spreading from the tip of the hairs on her head to the tip of her toes.

Several days went by before her mother, who felt a bit of com- passion for a moment, took Ana to the community hospital, which provided services free of charge. That hospital was a local clinic staffed by medical students completing their requirements for the university's school of medicine. After a preliminary checkup, the doctor noted two things: first, Ana's illness was not a case of any known strain of influenza, and secondly, Ana needed to go imme- diately to the university hospital where there were specialists. Those specialists, with more experience and training as well as having access to advanced diagnostic equipment, would be better able to assess Ana's condition, diagnose her illness, and prescribe the appropriate treatment regimen. By that time, a much weakened Ana had lost all sense of time and space. She did not remember arriving at the hospital or remember being taken to an examination room. She woke up to the reality of the emergency room as the medical staff inserted what seemed to be some huge needles into each arm. Each needle had a tube connected to a bag hanging from a pole at the head of her bed. Slowly a yellow liquid dripped from the bag into Ana's arm, stinging her arms where the medicine entered her veins. Ana begged them to stop the treatment. She felt that, rather than helping, the treatment was sapping her strength, and continued treatment would cause her to faint. The doctors, after discussing the treatment process and the symptoms felt that the illness must run its course. Telling both Ana and her mother, "We are sorry. There is not much that we can do in this case. This has no cure. You just need to take your daughter home."

With no money for a taxi, Ana's mother took her home on the bus. Ana did not realize how much time had passed between her leaving for the hospital and her return home. She only knew that she was horribly exhausted as she staggered to her room and fell asleep as soon as she lay down. She did not know how long she lay in a deep sleep, only knowing she was alive when the pain awakened her. After an indeterminate number of hours, she rose to a semi-conscious state but had a sense of the everyday world, a world of pain. As she lay in her bed awake or asleep, she traveled through a nightmarish landscape while seeing the world of the family as another universe fading in and out as she coped with her pain, anguish, and despair. Since her return from the hospital, no one came to her aid. Throughout her ordeal, nobody visited but a friend, who sat for a bit on the edge of her bed. Eventually, her friend left, padding softly into the distant haze surrounding Ana's world. Family members would look at her in passing. No one asked if she were okay or needed something to ease her pain or brought her anything to make her feel comfortable and alive. Innumerable days passed until Ana believed she could no longer endure the fever and pain that consumed every moment of every day. The nausea had become so bad that even water caused her to throw up. Ana was on the verge of both physical and spiritual collapse. All the light that always accompanied Ana had been extinguished. Ana, in coping with the illness that ravaged her body and her soul, turned to God and put her illness and suffering in God's hands with this simple prayer: "I don't know what punishment I'm paying for, and I apologize if I have done something to make me worthy of this punishment, but if you think there is still something, some service which I might serve in this life, please restore me. Take this pain from me and cease the torture I am being subjected to. If that is not your will, let me die now." After she finished her simple prayer, her thoughts turned to her family. Were they right about the university, that such a high calling was not for her, a calling that was too pretentious? If she were to quit her studies, give up her dream, her family would not stop ridiculing her but would continually confront her about the truth of their words.

That realization was almost as painful, if not more so, as the agony due to the illness. The thoughts of giving up only strengthened her resolve to continue the walk to better her life that begun with the best of intentions.

With that final thought, she drifted into a deep and peaceful sleep, at last free of the nightmares, her last thoughts being that she would never break the promise she made to herself when banishing any fears to God, into whose hands she had just given herself. As she slept, Ana felt her body begun to cool. In her dreams, she saw the remainder of her life enter a deep red tunnel. As she moved through the tunnel, her body slowly lost weight until it became weightless and seemed to float. There was a feeling of tranquility like she had never known before. In this world of reverie, there was no time or space. Later, Ana could only describe the sensation as similar to most people's concept of the infinite. As Ana moved deeper into the dream, she knew that the Almighty had heard her prayers, and he called her to himself. In doing so, he released her from her earthly struggles. The last section of her dream had her being carried away with feelings of peace and tranquility for an indefinite time. Into her realm of peace and tranquility, she heard a bird singing in the window. She was no longer at home because she knew no birds lived in her neighborhood, which was devoid of trees. As she looked toward the singling bird, the bright light of the rising sun shined on her face. She was alive; she had not been called to heaven. She knew that she had been returned to the reality of her former life to fulfill some yet unknown ministry. Above all, she was virtually free of the pain and fever that had wracked her body for days. Looking death, disguised as sickness, square in the eye and winning with the help of prayer and the Father was her experience and salvation.

As happy as she was to be cured, she first offered prayers of thanksgiving to God. Secondly, after her prayers, she tried to get out of her bed. She was finally able to stand and take a few shaky steps, but she did not reach the doorway before she fainted. Looking back, she does not recall falling to the concrete floor. When she regained consciousness, her mother was standing over her and asked why Ana was sitting on the ground rather than asking how she was feeling. Ana could barely answer her mother and murmured, "I was just resting." A few days later, as Ana began to regain her strength, she went to the local clinic/hospital, the same hospital she visited when she first became ill, to see if they could prescribe something to speed her recovery and improve her strength and energy. After examining her, the doctor told her no prescription medication was necessary. The only remaining symptom of her mysterious illness was weakness. The best medication, according to the physician, was to eat gelatin and oranges, primarily to recover her sense of taste, which she had lost. She was hungry but did not wish to eat much because she had no way of knowing if something were sweet or salty or acidic. However, three months later, by following the doctor's orders, Ana slowly began to recover her sense of taste.

When Ana became well enough to return to the university, she took advantage of a common and long-standing tradition of allowing students who had either not passed their end-of-semester exams for the second semester or who could not sit for the exams due to a major personal or medical problem to take them at their first opportunity. Retaking the exams was at the discretion of the individual instructors. Ana met with each of her instructors to request her retaking the exams, illustrating her request with details and summarizing her arguments as a case of major force. Her instructors, after some discussion among themselves, granted Ana permission to take the exams at the first opportunity. Ana was very grateful for the option, and desirous of maintaining her near perfect grade average, she focused on preparing for each test. Her hard work and conscientious preparation assured her passing all but one. That last test required an unusually high degree of reasoning, a skill with which Ana struggled as a side effect of her fever and attending illness. The teacher did not doubt that Ana was telling the truth; he noted her cadaverous face, emaciated body, and the strong caliber of her work before she became ill. To compensate for Ana's not passing the test, the professor assigned her a research project equal in difficulty to the exam. With its successful completion, Ana would complete the semester with her superior academic standing intact.

At the beginning of the first semester of her second term, Ana reviewed her finances and planned the whole school year. In addition to a tight budget, there was the shortage of both emotional and financial support from her family. To ease the tight financial situation and negate the drama at home and the tight finances, Ana decided to look for options rather than giving up. One alternative open to her was the university scholarship program for students with limited resources but with very good grades. Ana gathered the requisite paperwork and went to the rectory. That campus building held the offices at which students applied for grants and scholarships. She filled out the application and attached her scores from the previous school year. After all the applications were reviewed, the staff unanimously approved her request. For Ana, the news was like a glass of fresh water in the desert. Once awarded, her scholarship was renewable each semester. To retain the scholarship, Ana needed only maintain her current grades. With Ana's abilities, that was not a problem, and the financial security would lift a burden from Ana's shoulders and allow her to concentrate on her studies. Her grades were always at the top levels.

The only negative vibes of the second term came from the whines and complaints of her family and only intensified as Ana concluded the second year of her university studies. Throughout the year, there were the common sarcastic comments like, "Are you close to flunking?" The family unfailingly tried to break the persistence the drove Ana to succeed in university; it was an outgrowth of the persistence Ana exhibited prior to her enrolment. Ana's patented reply to the vitriolic babble was always, "Not yet until you drop!" A phrase often heard from Don Ira. Her mother would tempt her by saying "The door is wide open. I don't know what are waiting for." Over the midterm vacation, Ana began to think that the constant criticisms of her family might have reached a point at which she must either succumb to the weight of their comments and sarcasm or find a positive solution which would enhance her studies and her life.

Her first step toward improving her quality of life so she could be free of her family's toxic environment was to assess the cost of a room shared with another student or an individual room or apartment. After some searching, Ana did find a place in the center of the city. For Ana, who had never lived away from home, her new independent life was another challenge. Living completely alone, she would be without the familiar settings and without any support beyond God's blessings and her own abilities and drive. When Ana informed her parents about her plans to leave home, she expected nothing different from what she was accustomed to hearing. She was so right in her expectations. Her father, with his usual lack wit and selfishness replied, "As mochas, we noticed how smart you are and gave you a home, now you are going to pay rent to another damn ass."

Her mother chimed in with, "Good! Now you will know what it takes to keep up. Let's see if you can survive."

The brothers, not to be left out, chimed in, "Great! Now we no longer have to listen to this person who just annoys us with speeches of progress." With those blessings bestowed by her lovely family, Ana packed her bags, left home, and continued her adventures alone, at least for the time being.

THE NEXT CHALLENGE

*Freedom is a challenge that only belongs to those who
know how to earn it.*

Ana

She would leave nothing in the place Ana once considered her home. The first action in preparation to her leave-taking was to pack her few belongings from her small corner, which her family had allowed her to use. She had so few things that everything fit in a suitcase. She packed the copies of books and notebooks in a cardboard box and told the family that she would return for them later. She accepted the idea that no one would regret her leaving, and to test the idea, as well as tweaking her brothers' noses and in order to completely convince herself of her brothers' solidarity and their excitement at her departure, she asked if one of them would help her by carrying her suitcase to the bus stop. The brothers' reply was, "Wow, you can't even do that?" That convinced Ana that there were no ties binding her to this family, to that home. There was not one shred of evidence that even one family member cared, even just a little, about the years that she had tried to be part of the "happy family." She said nothing more, just picked up her suitcase and shook the dust from her feet as she closed the door and walked to the bus. She did not look back.

Ana rented a room from a family who posted an ad in the newspaper. What was missing from the ad was how nutty the family was. When Ana arrived they read their conditions, known as house rules, which for Ana, was not a big deal. After talking with the family and thanking them for the opportunity of living in their home, Ana politely excused herself. Being so tired, all she wanted was to sleep.

Ana moved to her room and lay on the bed, falling asleep almost immediately. Ana slept the rest of the day through and all through the next day too. Ana had not slept more than four or five hours per night for the last twenty years. Under her parents' roof, she was on call when her brothers were sick or when her brothers came home late from their many scandals and rowdiness to deliberately awaken her. She arrived at her new lodging sleep-deprived but did not know how much. Her landlords were very Catholic; there was not one Sunday on which they were not at Mass. The head of the house was a very respected artist for his skill in either designing or copying coats of arms. His wife believed she was very special because not only was she married to a highly talented and respected man but her father's family was well respected in the village from which she came. They had two boys and a girl. The children thought they were as intelligent as their father. When the family would attend Mass on Sundays, the children would complain with bloodcurdling cries and curses erupting like lightning and thunder in a hurricane. The walk home resembled the trip to Mass. Added to the children's outcries were their mother's grumbling comments about people who had attended mass and what had occurred or been seen on the journey home. Ana wondered if someone might have cast a spell on her. In many ways, there was no major difference between her birth family and the new family she was living in. After a very short stay, unable to stand the chaos and the confusion, Ana began to look for another place to live.

Between working part-time and completing the university studies, Ana managed to find another place to live. When she had secured the new rooms with some students, she gave notice to the family that she had found another place and that she would move out at the end of the month. They said that they were sorry to see her leave but would part on good terms. A month after moving, Ana received a phone call from her previous landlord. The artist asked Ana to meet him at a nearby coffee shop because he needed to talk with her. After they met and were seated, he confessed that his wife was jealous of Ana. He next advised Ana to be careful of the girls with whom Ana now lived, as they had very bad reputation. When pressed for examples of the girls' bad actions, the artist could give no credible examples. At that point in the conversation, with the question mark clearly visible on her face, Ana stood up and apologized for leaving so abruptly, as she had a very busy day. As she left the coffee shop, Ana again concluded that madness was not a trait reserved only to the poor.

In the new residence were four other girls. The oldest was in her forties and felt that, at her age, it was already too late to be fishing for a groom. She was satisfied with dating a man, whether he was married or not. The second roomer was a maiden girl of thirty-eight who, like the first roomer, thought that she had missed the train. She had two boyfriends, comparing their offerings to see which one would offer marriage. To enhance her chances of choosing appropriately, she decided to date both on the same day. She set her plan in motion by setting a time and place at which each was to meet her. One would pick her up at home at 5:00 p.m. and the other would meet her at 8:00 p.m. The first one came late while the second one arrived early. When the trio met in the rendezvous, the boyfriends knew that they had been played and accused her of being a cheater, a two-timer. After the guys verbally accosted her and became somewhat physical, the young lady made her choice. As a result of the confrontation and the conduct of each suitor, she cited the incident as the easiest way for her to choose the best suitor, as she later told the other roommates though not fully explaining the logic of her choice. As Ana listened, she could make little or no sense of the discussion and her reasoning.

The other two girls said they were sisters but bore little resemblance to each other. What they did together other than sleeping in the same room was to go dancing on Saturday night. On Sunday morning, they looked as if they had been hit by a train and did not know where they had left their underwear. Those behaviors were difficult for Ana to understand for several reasons. First, Ana had no time for a boyfriend and just ignored the boys who constantly asked her for a date. Secondly, she just could not understand why the sisters were not ashamed of their Saturday night activities. Ana eventually became the constant butt for the sisters' criticism because they could not relate to Ana's ideas and actions as much as Ana could not relate to theirs. Finally, one of them became pregnant, forced her boyfriend to marry her, and moved from the residence. Sometime later, the second supposed sister likewise became pregnant, forced her boyfriend to marry her, and moved out for the same reason.

The lady who shared the room with Ana was older and even more eccentric. She would watch Ana when she entered the room after a long day at work and school. The roommate would sit in front of her mirror and watch Ana through the mirror. Ana, coming home tired, would take her shoes off and her clothes and rest in her bed in her underwear. After partially undressing, Ana would rest her feet on the wall because her feet were very painful from her long day. When her roommate would see Ana almost naked, the lady would start crying and hurriedly leave the room. Ana was afraid to ask her roommate the reason for that odd behavior. However, the house mother, the lady in charge of the rooms, told Ana that the roommate was depressed, and seeing Ana, who was both young and physically fit, made the older lady sad. One day, when Ana returned from work, she saw posted directly in front of her bed a large picture of her roommate as a young woman. Ana acted as if she did not see the photograph and continued her routine while the lady again left the room weeping. A few days later, Ana came home from work to discover that the lady moved out. The landlord told Ana that the older lady could no longer endure Ana's daily routine.

Days went by, each blending into the next, and Ana continued her struggle to survive both school and work. Some days, she only had time to eat two meals, but she was as determined as ever to reach her goal, a university degree. The first day of her final year at the university began with Ana exceedingly nervous for three reasons. First, she was about to achieve one of her major goals, which was graduating from the university, and she did not want to falter on her journey with the end in sight. The second concern involved her career opportunities after graduation and a real fear of not finding a good job. The third worry was related to her birth family. To her way of thinking, she owed the family a debt. Although she was not living with her family, she felt guilty for not repaying the family what they might have sacrificed for her. To deal with her feelings of debt and guilt, Ana decided to visit her family to see how they were surviving. As she stepped through the door, the wailings of poverty and famine were as loud as ever. Ana realized that nothing had changed. With her or without her, the misery and deprivation still lived in her old home. Her family told her that living in such a horrendous place was no place to live peacefully. The family spoke of a huge increase in the crime rate; they spoke of girls becoming pregnant at twelve and teenagers drugging themselves with everything that was put in front of them. It was a neighborhood in which husbands left their wives for younger, better-looking women. For Ana's family, there was the additional stress caused by Don Ira often chatting with the neighboring prostitute. Needless to say, that was not really appreciated by his wife Igna.

Ana, taking pity on her parents and forgetting all the humiliations and bad moments she experienced in that house, asked her father how she could help a little. Her father, Don Ira, explained that under the circumstances, he had to find another neighborhood to build a safer home. As she said later when asked why she offered help and how much was needed to buy it, Ana said it was out of the kindness of her heart. When Don Ira told her the cost of building and resettling in a much better neighborhood, the amount represented more than half of Ana's savings than she hoped to use for her graduation fees and the costs of her diploma's paperwork. As she listened, she measured her father's needs against her own needs. Her desire to help and to reward her parents for the little that they had given while she lived with them proved to be the greater need. Ana decided to give her father most of her savings, keeping only enough to meet her own necessary requirements for the next few months. Don Ira was thrilled to accept the money and quickly purchased a new plot of land in a popular, up-and-coming community. Each family member held out hope that their new neighborhood was not as full of crime as the one they currently lived in. After giving her father her savings, Ana bid her parents farewell and returned to her home. Knowing that her savings had been drawn down, Ana worked even harder out of the fear that she might not have enough money to complete her studies. Taking a deep breath from time to time, Ana renewed her faith that everything would work out since she had made her decisions with her heart *and* her mind.

THE FINAL TEST

As her final year at university came to an end, a year highlighted by her giving money to her parents, Ana completed her undergrad studies through her persistence and ability. After graduation, she took a job at the Electoral College and decided to use the opportunity to complete her thesis project entitled "The National Census" prior to elections and its discrepancies. Ana's first job in government was as an electoral validator; it was a job secured through the recommendation of one of her teachers who was served as the president of the Electoral College. In the course of her work and with the help of some friends, she could work and complete her thesis project. Once completed, she could submit the thesis to her committee of judges for approval and awarding of her undergraduate degree.

Having faith in her abilities and education coupled with her ever-present hope, Ana continued working on the thesis project begun during the last year of the university. With hope in the fore and a bit of fear lurking in the background, Ana presented her thesis to the committee's evaluator, who accepted it. After review, he approved it, personally congratulating her for her solid thorough research, logical analysis, and strong writing. The oral presentation of the thesis was done before three judges, whom Ana had previously paid for the simple act of listening to the presentation. Ana made the necessary arrangements and prepared for the presentation, which would last at least an hour.

The highly anticipated date and time for her thesis presentation arrived, her moment of truth as Ana described it. Between giving her thesis to her teacher and the presentation, Ana had lost several kilos of weight due to stress and nerves. She knew she had to be at her best to cap off all the efforts and finally graduate. Daily, Ana prepared her presentation, refining it as much as possible. As she made her preparations, her primary concern was that no one would prevent her from completing her mission and from graduating successfully.

On the appointed place and at the appointed hour, Ana appeared before the judges and nervously began the presentation. Each judge had a copy of her thesis. Each of the judges would choose their questions from both the thesis and the oral presentation. They would ask their questions at the end of her presentation. Ana began her speech somewhat fearfully but confidently. Her reading was clear, emphasizing the points that needed emphasis and using her tone of voice to show relationships in the oral presentation. Instead of letting her speak for the usual hour as originally set for the presentation, the judges stopped her at the forty-five minute mark. The judges immediately began their barrage of questions to which Ana replied confidently and without hesitation. After seeing her command of the material and her ability to field their questions, the panel unanimously agreed to end their inquisition and to excuse her from her presentation. As she exited the chamber, she met other university students, curious to know the verdict. Ana did not immediately answer; she just did not know the answer. Ana's hands were sweaty, and she felt very light-headed and faint. After fifteen minutes of deliberation by the judges, the same fifteen minutes of anxiety for Ana, one the judges opened the door invited her to be seated in the chamber to listen to the verdict. Finally, Ana heard what she hoped to hear, "Congratulations, licensee! You have passed your professional exams and become a certified professional. You have also met all requirements for the undergraduate degree for a license in political science and public administration."

Those words were heavenly music to her ears. Joy overwhelmed her completely. She felt her heart throbbing so strongly that she thought it would jump out of her chest. Ana had conquered the first major hurdle on her road to success by completing the first licensure of her career. As she took time to breathe and calm her heart, Ana, following the custom of graduate students who pass their final requirement, invited the judges/teachers to dinner. To cover the costs, Ana withdrew the rest of the money from her savings account after issuing her dinner invitation. In a surprising turn of events, the judges volunteered to pay for the expensive dinner. As she left the academic halls, one other judge volunteered to drive her home. Ana was wary of the proffered kindness. She was unsure of the offer's authenticity but still accepted the favor. As they were driving, the teacher commented that when he had graduated he had celebrated the whole night with his friends. Ana, feeling the indirect, or possibly very direct, hint/invitation carried more than it stated, became somewhat nervous until she remembered that her friends were already waiting at her home to celebrate. The teacher said no more on the subject, which greatly lessened Ana's concerns. Perhaps there was no ill intent implied, or he knew that Ana was not like some of the girls who had recently graduated. At her door, he took her hand before departing and said, "I wish you the best in your new journey." With those words, he walked back to his car and drove off.

The graduation ceremony would be held the week following her oral presentation in a hacienda on the outskirts of the city. The recently graduated students had hired a band and a banqueting service. To cover expenses, each student was assessed a fee, the cost of an admission ticket for the number of guests invited by each graduate. Although Ana knew what her family thought of her achievement, she still bought ten tickets so her whole family could enjoy the ceremony and the feast. Still glowing from the happiness and satisfaction of graduating, she went home to inform the family of her having finally completed her university studies. Upon her arrival, she told them of her success and showed her parents the invitation and accompanying tickets for the dinner celebration. Her elation was short lived and the fire of her ardor was smothered by a wet-blanket reception. Her mother would not even look at the invitation, would not even congratulate Ana. She took a deep breath and quickly recovered her positive outlook and excitement. Nothing could smother for long. Joy filled Ana from head to toe. Her response to her mother's inaction and subsequent dismissal was to leave the invitation on the table and return to her own home.

On graduation day, Ana, hoping against hope, yet knowing her family very well, did not expect anything other than her family's indifference, disgust, and absence at the big event. The gifts from family were already given on more than one occasion. On that day of days, Ana was not disappointed. On that day of days, the ceremonies celebrated the graduates' achievements with families and friends joining in their loved ones' joy. The parents and friends of Ana's fellow graduates arrived with gifts and flowers. One parent even bought a car for his daughter. Ana watched from the sidelines with a bit of envy, as most of her fellow classmates shared the company of at least one friend. In a moment when no one would notice her, Ana left the party to shed a few tears alone then dried her eyes and returned to the group. When she returned to the party, she was relieved that no one questioned her absence. She again called on her inner strength and disguised her sadness behind a mask and remained at the party, acting as if nothing had happened.

A few days later, when the elation subsided somewhat, Ana began to look for work in areas of government other than the one in which she worked. She thought that by listing her university diploma on her resume, it would not be difficult to find a job worthy of her education. Unfortunately, Ana found the search more difficult than she originally thought. She learned that there were two requirements that she had not yet met. First, she needed political connections, and she had none. In addition, there were, as always, levers to access the political connections. The second requirement was the need for on-the-job experience, and her only experience was in social service. To offset these missing pieces, she requested a recommendation from one of her teachers, which only gave her a volunteer position, working without pay in the delegation of programming and budget. For a few months, Ana worked for them and learned that the only way for a female to climb the political ladder was to be "affectionate" with those who occupied a position of power and prestige in politics. Ana's next lesson came as she learned that she would have to wait many years to achieve a decent and worthwhile position in politics. Ana, though somewhat discouraged by those obstacles, did not lose her faith and hope in a brighter, successful future. One day, in a conversation with a few friends, Ana expressed a long-held desire to explore new worlds and new careers. One of her friends said that she had relatives in the United States of America. The idea of leaving all she had known to journey to another world, to take up another challenge in another country, sparked the flame of interest and further exploration. The idea of moving north so intrigued Ana that she looked for a paying job to offset her moving expenses and soon found a job in a department store. With her dream in the forefront, she saved enough money to cover minimal needs, packed her suitcase with only minimal necessities, and took flight northward to start a new odyssey.

BALANCE OF LIVED EXPERIENCES

All those who have tried to destroy my strength of will,
my spirit and my soul, see me yet standing
complete and calm.

Ana

I have written this book with the idea of eliminating or clarifying the many doubts of those who have ever questioned the direction my life's journey. All those who understand my aims in writing the book found stories and anecdotes that people around me thought I would not remember or would not wish me to tell. I hope that my family, through this book, now has a clear idea that things happen for a reason, and that some events can change a person's life. In my narrative, you, the reader, will find many memories that shaped my destiny, my personality, and my success if you would but see.

Notes to My Father

I would like to remind my father that although it is true that life is not a bed of roses, it is not a bed of pure thorns either. God and Mother Nature gave to us human beings certain attributes that no other living beings of the planet Earth have. These attributes include the proper use of the mind, including the ability to think, to reason, and hold the information we have gained in memory. Human beings have emotions which allow us to express anger, love, and joy to our fellow human beings in the world in which we live. We also have what many call the soul and spirit. All these attributes, when well used, will help a person transform the environment and convert the thorns to roses or, at least, to grow them to ease your suffering. This body that you, my father and mother, provided me whether by accident or through curiosity was not something you planned. It was Mother Nature's creation that God decided you should bring to this world. As a result, I free myself from any blame of my creation. In this full pardon, I include the guilt of being born female and the guilt of not being born with the features that you would have wished. If there is still some doubt in your part of my coming to be, you only need take a moment of your time to analyze the situation and circumstances of how I was created, and there you will find the answer to your questions. I came to the conclusion rather early in life that being born female does not make me either less or more than any other human being. While I am not more than everything else, I am thankful to Mother Nature and the universe for allowing me to exist here as long as God has allowed me. Life has placed many challenges before me from the moment of my birth, but it has also put me in touch with resources necessary to deal with them and, in most cases, to overcome them. Every challenge represents an opportunity to seize the moment in which God has allowed me to live and exist. You have said that I should show appreciation for what you and my mother called giving me life. I just want to remind you that a person is grateful for that which is given in goodwill or in good faith, not by accident, not by the union of two bodies when neither of whom ever thought that a baby would come from such a union. I could not show appreciation when I have been constantly reminded throughout my life that what was expected of the pregnancy was in the making a little man. I find giving appreciation difficult when you throw in my face your oft stated, very dreamy phrase, "God gives children to those who deserves them," referring in your thinking to the female giving birth only to sons. Even at this age, I try to remember the good things to be able to thank you. For some reason, beyond my understanding, I cannot remember anything that makes me feel very thankful. I can recall a phrase you, with much authority in your voice, often repeated to all of us, "My whole life would not be enough to thank my parents for what they have done for me." If I still owe you something, please tell me. I would like to know what the price would be then I can pay it to you, so it would be like your saying, "Cleared the accounts, now lasting friendships." I have put forth a great effort to remember your good deeds, but I think only of living in a house of wood with holes that the raw winter wind and rain penetrated. I think of hard ground that we had to sweep only to cover with rags and *paistle* to make a bed. I think of moldy green tortillas and weevil-infested beans that we were forced to eat when the situation became difficult and you sought no solution. I think of being forced to work to deserve even a roof over my head and the scraps of food given to a girl so young and who had never asked to come into this world. I think often of wearing rags and sandals with nails that made my feet bleed. I do have to thank both God and life, for they granted me the willpower to survive. It is with deep sadness I say this, "I would like to have a list of the good deeds to be able to show you here, but as I never received any, I can only lay before you a fraction of what I remember. I look back on your style of discipline and remember well your phrase, "Who does not execute children is because he does not love them." I have news for you. The use of brute force comes when the words cannot be called upon. As far as I remember, you never had the courtesy, or perhaps the thoughts or vocabulary, to explain the reason for your punishments. The weapon of choice, your belt, left marks that clipped my skin and which caused me much shame when I had to go to school with my legs marked by the execution, for things as simple as asking for a taco or taking a break from your forced tasks. Father, I hope that your children have given you all the satisfaction of which you once dreamed, from bales of money to the affection of your siblings who are no longer alive. Finally, I recall your words, "Educate your kids by example." I hope that none of them resolved their problems by beatings and abusive treatment of any type. I hope they provide their families with a decent roof, decent shelter, basic footwear, balanced nutrition, and balanced education wrapped in friendly and realistic communication. I hope they give their families unconditional love and a guided, optimistic expectancy for the life they lead. I hope they travel a road without reproach or culpability born out of your own disappointments.

To My Mother

I am forever grateful to you, my mother, for the gift of letting me develop in your womb and for not aborting me before my birth. I thank you for taking care of me, of giving me food after long hours of waiting in the cradle, and not letting me die of starvation. I thank you for changing my rags you called diapers when I was dirty and for healing me when I became ill despite being the infant who did not deserve your time. I believe those favors were paid for by taking care of the majority of my brothers in the same way. I could not thank you for hurting me by not seeing me as an important part of your life other than as a working tool or a slave. Neither could I thank you for your disappointment, for not being born with white skin, blue eyes, and curly blonde hair. You clearly told me that I defrauded you. I just want to make it clear to you that neither you nor your husband chose or have the genes you expected to see in your children nor the order in which you passed them on to your children. I release myself, therefore, from any responsibility, being the whole person I am. I had no choice in the two people who created me either by accident or by reasons yet unknown. As for the problem of your varicose legs, blame for which you lay on me, I remove myself from such responsibility or from whatever happened while I was not even born. I could not control my diet during my manufacturing process. Taking a moment to dig deeply into my memories, I have found something to thank you for in reference to some prejudices. Thank you. Without knowing it or without consciously thinking of it, you sowed fear in me. That fear helped me to err in my social interaction, especially in succumbing to negatives that grew from what others said or did. Fear kept me focused first on escaping from so much ignorance by using the information and experiences provided by my early teachers. Education framed my thoughts toward finding ways to change the future.

Utilizing education as the first step to escape from the nightmare in which I was living was the force behind my escaping to the classroom without having been registered in school. I believe that the teacher knew I was not registered, but he showed no anger or contempt when I quietly arrived in his room with my own bench to sit at the back of the classroom, so as not to interrupt the class. It never mattered that I later received a beating at home by having gone to the street. Mother, I do not want you to take that behavior or my next comments as an insult but only as truths hidden from your society. I definitely want to tell you that life is so much more than thinking about who is going to accept you as his wife or as his companion. I want to add that no woman has to bear all the children that your partner forces you to have. In the true union of marriage, the man must compliment who you already are. He must conquer the obstacles in life and love, and he must protect you. The relationship you and your husband built within your home depends on the quality of life, or lack of quality, that you give to your sons. The caliber of your relationship will write your destiny as a couple and, finally, as a family. Your children are not born to be objects of criticism or to be raised with the constant reminder that you gave them their life, and they have to pay for your gift to them. You must be reminded that your children are the result of what you wanted and what you chose. We all have choices in life, and daily, you choose your destination and mission in life. If you still have doubt of why I did not follow in your footsteps, I tell you clearly in a few simple words. First, I never met a man that I could like wholeheartedly—a man who is intelligent, educated, hardworking, and who is always thinking of a more promising future; who is and wishes to always be self-sufficient; and who is (why not) handsome. Such a man does not scare me. Yes, as I write this, I can see your expression as you note that I did not have all the beauty and intelligence to deserve a man with those traits. I would like to remind you or, perhaps, tell you for the first time, beauty is in the eyes of those who know how to see it under any circumstances—often said as being in the eye of the beholder. I hope that someday you can see something beautiful in your life that will help you to smile and say, "That was worth this life." Through my studies and life experiences, I have learned that the love and affection of a mother for all her children has no monetary price nor can be shielded by time or space. A mother's love is unconditional and voluntary. The love and acceptance that you give to your children, you give unconditionally and as a maternal instinct, not because you are born to do it or by some innate fear that your children can replace you with someone who is capable of giving maternal love. Another reason, perhaps the most important that I could give, is my desire for personal dignity and in thinking there is always a path to follow that is different from the path which another imposes upon you. In addition to finding and shaping my own way in life, it was very important for me to show you that a person can make her own life without reproducing or making families. It is much easier to play the game chosen for you and do what everyone else does than to open a path for your own life. If you need more proof that there are many paths to a fulfilling life, you need only look around a moment to see how many people are choosing the same path as their forefathers and are living the same lifestyle. Now look at them and tell me what you are seeing in them. You can, perhaps, see a pretended smile of happiness and satisfaction. However, as my eyes were opened by education and experience, what I saw more and more clearly were families who lived in squalor, lamenting their fate and destiny and doing nothing to change their lifestyle. Among those families, I see many faces that behind their smiles lurks a desire to have other options in life. However, these family members do nothing; they simply resign themselves to believing their lifestyle choice is the right decision because the choice makes their life easier. Abandoning their lives of squalor for the difficult road to opportunity would make life harder. These people are fooling themselves. It is not easy to accept the things that hurt you, and it is not easy to find the sufficient courage to change the things that hurt you. It is even more difficult to accept responsibility for the mistakes of the past. Failure on this step to change only means that the person must pay, often dearly, in the future for their inaction.

It is important to note here that rarely does someone, before leaving this world, escapes paying for the damage that they have done to others. I know that I am not a saint, but I could never imagine having children and allowing them to suffer what I suffered: neglect, physical and emotional abuse, as well as exploitation of the person, and the limitation of an infant's dream. I never see myself repeating the story of my early life. I never can picture a home in which the parents sleep in a bed with a mattress under warm blankets while the children sleep on the ground, covered only with rags and feeling a cold that reaches to their bones. I could never eat from a plate full of food while my children only have a plate full of small crumbs. These choices I make grew not from cowardice but grew from an awareness of humanity. I would prefer being judged a thousand times by the ignorant for not being like them rather than to live a life in hardship and deprivation, lacking not only of the most essential goods but also the love and acceptance that are the main components of self-esteem. I would stifle any idea of thinking that one day I would become like them. My dream of living in my house without being in debt to anyone always made me fight more diligently against everything I saw while growing up. The idea of being something more than a baby factory or a source of someone else's satisfaction grew inside me as strongly as the need to breathe. As I watched the world around me and gained an education, I found the answers to many of my questions and, why not say it, a much better way to live. I could list many more reasons why I chose a different the path and very different destination from the life you had set for me.

For now, I can put some of your fears to rest by clarifying for your peace of mind or consciousness to an unfounded fear that I can like men or not or concerns of my being a lesbian or not. I clearly tell you that although I will not be found in a magazine as a model, I feel very grateful that the body that nature gave me is well defined and, for your satisfaction, is quite feminine and so is my mind. In another note, to allay your fears, you will never see me chasing the men as you expect because I don't consider such action necessary, especially when more than one has run after me. Just as you have chosen your lifestyle and have chosen the man with whom you had hoped to be happy according to your dreams, I too have chosen my path based on all that I saw at home and in my surroundings. Seeing your face full of concern, which I never forgot, brought me grief and sadness growing up and still does this day. I have no memory of ever seeing you smile, even with all the efforts that my brothers and I did to make you smile. I have always had the desire to ask if you were ever happy and what overshadowed your life. Seeing me reflected in your mirror chilled my blood. In addition to thinking that one day I would feel trapped in my own trap, a trap coming from being resigned to a life someone else could give me, made me feel as if I were drowning. Your bleak words, saying that a woman cannot survive without a man at her side burned into my soul like liquid fire on my skin. The fear of such a life was as strong as my fear of living in this world full of misery and ignorance. The doubt of what awaited me outside the world I knew made my legs tremble. Your discouraging reviews of my dreams and your guesses that I did not deserve anything in life, even men, since none would like me because I did not behave like other girls my age really made me feel as big as an ant. You fed my insecurity that was already overflowing my skin; my visible insecurity made me more vulnerable in the eyes of those who saw me as prey to be attacked so as to somehow satisfy their feelings of frustration toward life. I survived because, throughout, I believed that God is my grantor and guardian, who always protected me from predators and dangers that lurked around me, waiting to ruin the rest of my life. After having sought answers in the books and from the people who surrounded me, I can now better understand that there is no fault or sin from those around me to punish. The forces of destiny are as strong as my desire to make a mark in this life. This is something vastly different from what others expected of me. Once again, I must reiterate my belief that life does not only consists of having children or meeting someone. Life can offer a different path and a system for a better life other than the one someone had imposed on me by reciting that their version is my destiny. I hope someday you understand my way of thinking, and from the bottom of heart, I had a lifelong hope for nothing more than there be a connection between mother and daughter. However, even though I tried during my entire childhood and continued through a part of my youth, I could never effect that connection, and only God knows why. With no connection to parents, home, and family, I decided to leave the place that left so many marks on my history to start upon a new path on which only

God sees the destination. Embarking on my journey helps me feel alive. From my heart, I hope that you have found some happiness and satisfaction. I truly hope life has compensated you in some way for all of your investments and sacrifices. You probably thought that I am not a person to express what I have laid out in the previous lines but that does not surprise me in the least. I know that, just like my father, you always thought that I was a very insignificant person who was unable to open my own path in this life. I cannot even tell you what I thought of the system of life that you thought was correct. I do not remember having ever heard you giving me words of encouragement to make me think that I was on the right track or that I was wrong. In conclusion, I need to tell you again that I am not judging you. You probably did not know or did not want to know the value of a human being who is part of you. Perhaps, you just did not know the value of at least recognizing that your daughter is a human being. May God bless you.

To My Brothers

I give to my brothers an apology if ever I treated them harshly or unjustly. Mistreating you hurt me so much, but I was only following the behavior our parents sowed in my field. My intentions were to prevent you from repeating the same cycle of poverty, ignorance, and desolation in which you found yourself as children and teens. I understand that you had to defend yourselves, and in so doing, sometimes unfairly insulted me. Now I understand the force of the blood and genetics, something that opened my eyes to the world in which we grew up. I hope that those feelings, those experiences, and genetics do not affect your new families. Regarding your support, I have nothing to say. I think those omens which you so vehemently wished upon me and my future have borne results. To the blond person who always made fun of me for not being white and having a small nose, as well as making jokes about my "obesity" and lack of finesse, life repaid you with other disappointments and failures, which even you have not been able to see. As a reward for your vinegary demeanor, you married the son of a sex trader's "gallant life/madam" who did not know how many men had fathered her children. Your husband, who did not know who his father was, had several sisters in the "sex trade." Your husband could not treat you any differently than his parents, and to complete the picture of your downfall, sired a daughter for you exactly like him, a *panzoncita* or chubby, short, and with the mental impairments of the two. You had too many expectations, too many changes to keep up. Well, this is life. It always passes the bill and exacts payment in kind. To the next in line, my dear Chino, there is so much to say. Remember when I returned home very late from the preparatory school, nearly in the middle of the night. I had taken the latest bus and had no money to buy something for dinner before arriving home. Everyone had eaten and the casseroles were empty. There was nothing more than a package of tortillas in the fridge. When asked why there was not even a taco left on the plate, you faced me and jumped to the defense of the other members of the family. In your most sneering voice, you said that the other family members did not know what kind of monkey business I was involved in, but you did. Your closing remark was clear and simple, "You do not deserve even one taco!" My reply was to the point, "If I had been picked up from a dump, you might treat me this way, but not your sister!" You, defending our mother, said with so much authority, "Let her talk. When she comes out with a belly, she will have to eat her words and ask for forgiveness for such boldness." To which I replied you, "I hope you marry soon so that life will give you daughters, and everything you wanted for me today will come true but for you!" You experience your words, so you can know how I feel at this moment. You became very angry and yelled at me, "Now you shut up or I'll punch your face!" I replied, "Do it if you think it would save you from the fate that awaits you, the fate you just wished on me. Mark these words well! The more you continue punishing and abusing me, the greater your punishment will be." I do not have to remind you of what fate has given you. Twenty years after your outburst, life rewarded you with two little girls. The first, at exactly at seventeen years of age, the age at which you falsely prophesied my fate, gave you the big belly that you wished for me. To add insult to injured pride and bravado, your daughter's teacher was the father. Remember these words, the law of karma exists. To the poor guero who fought to defend his place as one of the male of the house and who between your rants and insults called me gay, who called me the culprit of your dating failures and the cause of your failing to earn a college degree, I tell you this, I did not have nor have I ever had any role in choosing your dates. You just did not have enough character to choose a good mate or complete a college degree. You and you alone are responsible for your disappointments in life. I am responsible for my success because I never gave up. I wear my responsibility like a garment. I am determined to be successful. I am proud to think I needed no one's approval or support to shape me as the person I have become. Your insults and the discouragement from the rest of my brothers have not broken me or my spirit. My strength to withstand is the victory that makes me no more or no less than any other woman. On the other hand, I can feel sorry that you have continued to eat the poop of your life. You started off as a baby who ate the poop from his diaper when your mother took long to change it. Such action, such trials are life, right? To the neutral one, I hope that you have decided on something in life because no one could live always being neutral. To Grumpy, I am glad you met a woman who controlled your anger and, in time, gave two children to entertain you. To the enlightened one, I hope that so much light does not blind you, so you will see the reality in which you live. Seeing clearly in the sunlight, you will provide a realistic education to the little enlightened *iluminaditos* entrusted to your care. To the gentle one, I wish you to find purpose in life. I hope you remain very righteous and you continue helping your parents by taking good care of their home. To the moreno, I wish you to continue to enjoy the happiness you described when you said you were "as happy as the day on which you were born." It is good that the bad moments have been deleted from your memory. To the cherub, I say that I am truly glad that you have found a hardworking woman who cares for you and makes your house a home.

A Look at the Sun

I do not ask for your help, because I know you will decline.

I just want you to respect my way of survival along the line.

By denying me your love, you tried to destroy my will.

Certainly, I tell you, try again and you will see.

What doesn't kill me can only make you stronger!

Just dare to challenge me, and I will rise luckier.

When you challenge my courage with hate, I await your attack every day.

I am the child of the rising sun, but the daughter of the morning I have been called.

When you want to look down at me, just look up at the horizon, for there I will be found.

Do not try to break my ego. Think before you act

If you want to play with fire, beware! The fire will burn you back.

Mariana

"I Wanted to Change the World"

When I was a young man, I wanted to change the world.
I found it was difficult to change the world,
so I tried to change my nation.
When I found I couldn't change the nation,
I began to focus on my town.
I couldn't change the town, and as an older
man, I tried to change my family.
Now as an old man, I realize the only thing I can change is myself,
and suddenly, I realize that if long ago I had changed myself,
I could have made an impact on my family. My family
and I could have made an impact on our town.
Their impact could have changed the nation, and
I could indeed have changed the world.
Unknown Monk, AD 1100